NASHVILLE – BOOK SIX – SWEET TEA AND ME

NASHVILLE – BOOK SIX – SWEET TEA AND ME

INGLATH COOPER

Contents

Books by Inglath Cooper

Copyright Trade Publishing

Published by Fence Free Entertainment, LLC
Copyright © Inglath Cooper, 2014
   Cooper, Inglath
   ISBN – 9781728904863

Fence Free Entertainment, LLC
Fence.free.entertainment.llc@gmail.com

Publisher's Note

This is a work of fiction. Names, characters, places, and incidents are a product of the author's imagination. Locales and public names are sometimes used for atmospheric purposes. Any resemblance to actual people, living or dead, or to businesses, companies, events, institutions, or locales is completely coincidental.

Thomas Franklin and Lila Bellamy have history. And now it seems, they may have a future as well. Or at least, a shot at one. Their second beginning though is anything but smooth. In the middle of the night, they flee Lila's hometown for Nashville, after stealing a dog in order to save his life. And if that's not a rocky enough start, they've got to figure out how to be the parents their daughter Lexie needs them to be, even as they acknowledge their growing feelings for each other.

Lila

The Kindness of Strangers

THE EMERGENCY VETERINARIAN services parking lot is empty except for one car. I'm thankful to see that it's not already full with other patients. I feel as if I've been holding my breath since the moment I heard the gun go off and realized Brownie had been hit, every second that passes making it less likely that he will survive.

The fear that has both Thomas and me in its grip is like a chokehold at our throats. Neither of us has been able to voice a word throughout the thirty-minute drive here. I send Macy a text and ask her if she can stay at the lake house with Lexie until we get back. I'm sure she thinks we're up to something very different from what we're actually doing, but I can't bring myself to try and explain right now.

Thomas has broken every speed limit along the way, and I've been praying one plea after another that we would get here without being pulled over.

He wheels the truck into a front spot and jumps out, opening the back door and carefully lifting Brownie off the seat. Brownie makes a small, whimpering sound. Thomas cradles him against his chest and walks quickly to the entrance door. I run ahead of them and open it, waiting just inside for the front desk attendant to buzz us in.

When she spots Brownie in Thomas's arms, she immediately picks up her phone and requests help from the back.

A young guy in blue scrubs pushes through a set of swinging doors off the waiting area and says, "Hey. I'm Jonathan. What happened?"

"He's been shot," Thomas says, his expression tight with worry.

Jonathan takes Brownie from him, and says, "We'll do our best," before walking quickly through the doors and disappearing from sight.

The woman at the front desk looks at us both with sympathy. "I'll need to get you to fill out some forms."

I step over to the desk and take the papers, looking at the information blanks and then at Thomas. He senses my unspoken questions and pulls a credit card from his wallet, handing it to the woman.

"We found him," he says. "But I want to take care of the bill."

"Oh," she says, uncertain. "Do you want us to call animal control for you?"

"No," he says quickly. "We'll wait here for him."

She squints a bit, as if she's not sure what to make of Thomas's story. But then she glances at the credit card, reads his name and says, "Oh, my goodness, you're Thomas Franklin. I love Barefoot Outlook!"

He smiles, recognizing the moment of leverage and says, "I really appreciate that. If you can just run my card for the charges, that would be great."

"Of course," she says, smiling at him now in a completely different way. She swipes the card through her machine, waits for the number to register and then hands it back to him. "I hope he'll be okay," she says.

"Me too," Thomas agrees with a nod.

"We can just wait on those forms," the woman says, looking at me now. I hand her the clipboard before she adds, "Y'all can wait over there. Someone will be out as soon as they know something."

"Thank you," Thomas says, rewarding her with one of his most memorable smiles. He takes my elbow, and we sit in a couple of chairs at the far end of the waiting area.

"I guess that fame thing comes in handy every now and then," I say.

"Every now and then," he says. His face is serious again, the smile he'd bestowed on the receptionist fading under his previous concern.

We sit, quiet for a few minutes, as if both of us are trying to absorb everything that's happened. I am the first to speak, my voice shaking as I ask, "Do you think he'll make it?"

"I don't know," Thomas says honestly, pain in his voice.

And that's when I start to cry again, the sadness rising up out of me with such immediate force that I have to cover my mouth to keep the sobs from breaking through.

He slips his arm around my shoulders and pulls me against him.

"How could he do that to an innocent dog?" I say.

He shakes his head, stiffening, and I can feel his disgust for Rowdy and everything he represents. "I guess I've got to believe justice wins out in the end," he says.

I turn my face to his chest, aware that my tears are soaking through his shirt, but I can't stop them. He rubs my back with one hand, and we just sit there, waiting, dreading what we might hear. We watch for someone to come out to let us know what's going on.

It's nearly an hour before the doors swing open again. This time, a man with white hair and kind blue eyes makes his way over to where we are sitting. "I'm Dr. Agnew," he says, shaking hands with us both and then taking the chair next to Thomas. "We were able to get the bullet in his shoulder out. We also stitched up the not insignificant number of bite wounds on his body. Mind if I ask how they got there?"

I can tell it's a question he's asked before. He's looking at us as if he suspects we are responsible for those wounds.

So I tell him what happened. "He doesn't belong to us. My neighbor put him in a dog fight tonight. We kind of intervened."

"Well, thank goodness for that," Dr. Agnew says, shaking his head. "Wounds of this sort and from that source rarely get treated by a vet."

"Will he be all right?" I ask.

"I hope so," the doctor says. "I've given him an injection of antibiotics, and he will need to continue with an oral dose for two weeks. We've already got that prepared for him."

"Okay," I say.

"May I ask what you're planning to do with him if he's not your dog?"

I look at Thomas, realizing I haven't thought a moment beyond finding out whether Brownie will live.

Thomas speaks first. "We can't let him go back to his owner. He'll probably shoot him on sight."

Dr. Agnew frowns and says, "Maybe you shouldn't tell me anymore."

Just then the front door buzzes, and a county deputy sheriff walks in. He nods in our direction and heads over to the receptionist to ask her something.

Dr. Agnew stands and says to Thomas and me, "If you could come with me for a moment."

We follow him through the swinging doors, and I immediately spot Brownie on a stainless steel table, still unconscious.

"I would guess that deputy is here about this situation. I have no desire to get on the wrong side of the law, but it would be my suggestion that you take the dog and leave now. The last case I had like this, the county insisted that the dog be euthanized because it had been part of a fight ring."

My heart thuds so hard in my chest that I immediately feel sick. "What?"

"Let's go before this turns into something we can't fix," Thomas says quickly. "Is there a back entrance, Dr. Agnew?"

"Yes, just down that hall," he replies, pointing to show us.

"I've already given the receptionist my credit card," Thomas says, reaching in his pocket and pulling out his keys.

The doctor nods. He hands Thomas the medication to give to Brownie, explaining how to take care of him for the next several days. "Thank you."

"No, thank you," he says, handing the keys to me. "Can you get the truck and pull around back? I'll meet you there with Brownie."

"Okay," I say, and on impulse, step forward to hug Dr. Agnew. "Thank you so much."

"You're welcome," he says, his expression softening. "Thank you for what you've done for him."

Without giving myself time to think, I walk quickly out the doors and through the waiting area, not looking at the deputy. I can feel myself shaking, my legs so weak I'm not sure I'll make it to the truck. But I do, and I force nonchalance into my efforts to open the door, slide into the driver's seat and back out of the parking space. I drive slowly around back, weak with gratitude when I spot Thomas standing there with Brownie in his arms.

He places him gently on the back seat and then climbs in the passenger side, his voice low and urgent when he says, "Let's go."

I pull out of the parking lot and onto the main road. It isn't until we reach the Interstate, and I have merged into the middle lane, speedometer on sixty, that I actually allow myself to breathe.

♪

Thomas

Dream Come True

LILA KEEPS THE truck right at the speed limit until we are out of the city and back on county roads. She drives a little faster then, as if she's as anxious as I am to leave behind the deputy and the risk he presented to Brownie.

We don't say anything for the first several miles, and when I speak, I can hear a slight tremor in my voice. "That could have been really bad," I say.

Lila grips the wheel tightly and nods. "I know. What if Dr. Agnew had—"

"He didn't though. We lucked out with a good guy."

"Does he look okay?" Lila asks, glancing over her shoulder at the back seat and then at the road.

I turn in my seat and watch Brownie for a moment before saying, "I think so. He's breathing."

A little while ago, that wasn't necessarily a given.

"Thank you, Thomas," she says now. "For getting him here. And for taking care of the bill. I'd like to help with—"

"Hey," I say. "There's no need for that."

"But it's not fair to saddle you with all of it—"

"I want to pay for it."

She sighs as if she knows arguing is futile. "Thank you," she says again. We're silent for a moment before she adds, "How did you get to be such a good guy?"

"I have my moments on the other side of the fence," I say.

"It's kind of hard to picture you there."

"At one time, isn't that exactly where you saw me?"

She glances at me, twists her palms on the steering wheel and says, "I don't think I was fair to you."

"Can I be honest?"

She nods.

"I don't either."

"I was just scared, Thomas."

"I know. But what if I hadn't come to Roanoke for that show? Would you ever have told me about Lexie?"

She stares at the road ahead, bites her lip, and then in a soft voice, admits, "I really don't know the answer to that."

We let the admission hang there in the dark between us, the truck engine the only sound in the silence.

"You have to admit we made a pretty good team tonight," I finally say.

"Yeah. We did."

"We have a daughter to raise, Lila. We have a daughter. I don't have a crystal ball, so I can't tell you exactly how this will all play out. But I want to be a part of giving her a good life."

"I know you do."

"Are you going to let me?"

She doesn't say anything for several long moments, but then nods, as if there is no other possible answer for her to give.

I glance back at Brownie again. "They're likely to come looking for him at the lake house."

"I've already thought about it," she says, the words unsteady.

"We should get him out of the area."

"I know."

"How do you think he'd like living in Nashville?"

"I imagine he would like it just fine."

"How would you like living in Nashville?" I ask in a softer voice.

"I once dreamed of living there," she admits, not looking at me, but straight ahead at the road.

"Wanna make that dream come true?"

"You're not an easy man to say no to, you know that?"

"I kind of pride myself on that particular point," I say, feeling lighter suddenly than I've felt in a while.

"Are you sure we can make it work?" she asks, still without looking at me.

"I think two people who want something badly enough can absolutely make it work."

"I gave up being a dreamer a long time ago, Thomas."

"This isn't a dream, Lila. It's the real thing. Can you trust me on that?"

She does glance at me then, and I can see in her face how much she wants to do just that. At the same time, I know how many times she's been let down in her life by people she loved and trusted.

"It'll take some time," I say. "But I'll prove it. You'll see."

She smiles a little then and nods once. I'd like to think she believes me, but I think in truth, words will only go so far.

I have a lot more for Lila than words.

♪

Lila

Until

FEW THINGS IN my life have ever felt harder than leaving Macy behind.

It's after four a.m. when we get back to the lake house. Thomas tells her everything that happened while I go to check on Lexie. When I walk back into the kitchen, I can see he has already told her of our plans to go ahead and leave for Nashville.

Her eyes fill with tears, but she walks over and hugs me hard, saying, "That's where you need to be. It's where you needed to be all along. No big surprise that it took a dog to convince you."

I start to laugh, but it comes out as a sob, and we stand there crying and hugging.

"We'll have plenty of room if you'd like to come too, Macy," Thomas says above our sobbing.

Macy pulls back to look at me. "Could he be any more of a keeper?"

"I'm serious, Macy," he says. "It's a good town. Bet you'd like it."

"How about I promise to visit soon?" she says, brushing away my tears with the back of her hand.

"It won't be soon enough," I say.

She takes my hand, and we walk to the bedroom where she helps me pack what few things I have here.

"You're not planning to go back to your place to get stuff, are you?"

"I don't know if I should—"

"You definitely should not," Macy says. "In a few days when Rowdy's had time to cool off, I'll go out there and pack up your things and ship them to you."

"You're an incredible friend," I say and step forward to hug her again.

"Hey, this isn't good-bye," Macy says. "Just until."

"Promise you'll come visit really soon?"

"You know it."

"Am I doing the right thing, Mace?"

"You want my honest answer?"

"Of course."

"Then yes. For you. And for Lexie."

"How could I have thought he wouldn't want to know her?"

"You were protecting her, Lila. Who can blame you for that?"

"It turns out I almost deprived her of a father."

"That child has been anything but deprived of love. Only now, she'll have more. And you can never have too much love."

"I love you, Mace."

"I love you, Lila."

"Promise me you'll be good to yourself?"

"Promise," she says.

♪

IT FEELS LIKE I'm in a dream.

I'm awake, but with every mile we leave behind, I wonder exactly what it is we're headed for. Difficult as my life has been at times, it is a life I know and have managed to deal with, make peace with.

What's ahead, I can only imagine. But nothing about it seems real. It's as if I am trying to picture someone else's life, and that I'll be trying to make it fit Lila and me when there's actually no size that will work for us.

We've just crossed the state line into Tennessee when Thomas looks at me and says, "Don't think about it too much. You'll make it far scarier than it's really going to be."

"It is scary though."

"Different. But nothing to be scared of."

I glance back at Lexie, asleep in her seat. Brownie is still unconscious under the effects of pain medication, but his head is right next to her arm, and every once in a while, she reaches out to rub him.

"I'm taking her away from everything she knows," I say. "What if she's scared?"

"She might be at first. But we'll do everything we can to help her get adjusted quickly."

We drive on for a bit without talking. "Thomas?"

"Hmm?"

"I don't really know how to say this because everything is so unclear right now. But I don't expect you to take care of me. Lexie is one thing—"

"Hey. I understand why you feel that way. But if there's anything good about what I've accomplished over the past few years, it's being able to help out the people I care about when they need help."

I look at him then, feeling a deep connect of something that I am reluctant to identify. I put teasing in my voice when I say, "Does that mean you care about me?"

He looks at me then, and there's not a speck of teasing in his voice when he says, "Yeah. That's exactly what it means."

It's like playing with fire, and I know it. I know in my heart that I have to make Lexie's well-being first and foremost in my relationship with Thomas. Flirting with him when I've already told myself it could end badly is probably not the direction I should be taking.

Am I attracted to him? Without doubt. Who wouldn't be attracted to him?

Do I want the best for our daughter? Without question.

He's asked me to trust him. And I want to. But the truth is I'm not so good at trusting. I'm really good at imagining all the things that can go wrong. I guess I have the experience to back that one up.

If it goes wrong for me, that's one thing. But messing things up for Lexie? That's a place I can't go.

♪

Thomas

For Real

IT'S LATE AFTERNOON when we pull into the circular driveway of the house I bought last year in an upscale Nashville neighborhood. The community is mostly made up of other artists, producers and songwriters.

Holden and CeCe live a few blocks away. I liked the idea of living near them because, to be honest, separating from them was pretty much how leaving home for college had felt. They're my extended family, and it's nice to know they're not far away.

At the time I purchased the house, it seemed crazy big with rooms I would never use. A pool out back. An enormous fenced backyard. But now, with Lila and Lexie here with me, I'm suddenly glad for all of it. Glad to have something like this to share with them.

"Wow," Lila says, staring at the house from the front seat of the truck. "It's incredible."

"I knew it was too much for just me, but the neighborhood feels safe. And the gated part is good."

"Yeah," she says. "I imagine you get some overzealous fans now and then."

"Not that often," I say. "Most people are good about respecting personal space."

"Macy saw Kenny Rogers in this restaurant one time," Lila says. "He was sitting at a table by himself, and this woman went over and sat down with him. Right next to him. And she wouldn't quit talking. Macy said you could see how hard he was trying to be polite, but the woman really deserved for him to be rude to her."

I shrug. "I feel his pain. You kind of hate to shut people down when they've bought your music and come to your concerts."

"Everybody has their limits though."

"Yeah. By the way, is this what you call a delay tactic? Talking instead of going in?"

Lila smiles a little and says, "Maybe."

"The house is actually friendlier than it looks."

"It is a bit intimidating."

"Well, come on," I say, opening the truck door and getting out. "Let's get you introduced."

I pull Lexie's chair from the back and walk around to pick her up and lower her into it. She's been asleep, and she rubs her eyes with the back of her hands, yawning.

Lila takes over then, pushing the chair around the front of the truck while I walk to the other side and lift Brownie out of the seat. I remember the house keys then and ask Lila to fish them out of my pocket.

She does so while we both try to look nonchalant. But her cheeks are red, and she doesn't look at me as we walk to the front door. She inserts the key, and the door swings in. "Here we are," I say.

"Oh, my goodness," Lila says, letting her gaze take in the vast foyer with its tumbled marble floor, the long hallway that leads to the kitchen and open living area.

"How about let's get Brownie settled, and I'll show you around?"

"Sounds good," she says, still looking awestruck.

"There's a room off the kitchen that includes a dog door. It opens into the fenced back yard. The previous owner had dogs, and it comes in handy when Hank Junior and Patsy are visiting. It will make it easier for Brownie to come and go as he pleases, as soon as he's feeling better."

"He won't know what to make of this life. Actually, I'm not sure any of us will."

I find some quilts in a linen closet and we make a bed for Brownie. He's groggy, but whines a little and licks my hand once, before lowering his head and closing his eyes.

"Your heart just melted, didn't it?" Lila asks with a smile.

"A little," I admit. "Okay, a lot."

We look at each other then, awareness of everything that's happened in the past twenty-four hours hanging there between us.

"I'm also not sure how any of us will ever thank you."

"You don't need to thank me," I say. "I'm happy you're here. All three of you."

"Have you thought about how devastating we're going to be to your bachelor routine?"

"It actually got pretty lonely around here at times," I admit. "I've never liked living alone."

"You might change your mind on that after a while," she says.

"I don't think so," I say.

We study each other for a few long moments, and I want in the worst kind of way to pull her into my arms and kiss her. But at the same time, I don't want to mess any of this up. So I step back, blow out a deep breath and say, "Let's show Lexie her room and see what she thinks of it."

"Okay," Lila says, nodding once without meeting my eyes.

And I'm pretty sure she wanted me to kiss her just as much as I wanted to do so.

♪

Lila

Only in Magazines

I'VE NEVER EVEN been in a house like this.

I've seen pictures of them in magazines, but they didn't seem real. More like something from a movie set, maybe. A pretend place where pretend people live.

My bedroom connects with Lexie's. There's an enormous bathroom between the two with double sinks, a gigantic walk-in shower and heated floors.

Lexie takes it all in with wide eyes, as if she isn't sure what to make of any of it. She stares at me and then tears slide from her eyes, trailing down her cheeks in telltale evidence of her uncertainty.

"Oh, baby," I say, not sure how to even start explaining it to her. I kneel beside her chair and take one of her hands in mine.

"I know this is confusing, sweetie. The truth is I should have told you about Thomas a long time ago. I'm sorry that I didn't. If I had, maybe this wouldn't feel so strange right now."

Lexie leans forward and wraps her arms around my neck, holding on as if I am the only known in her existence. And in this new life we're seeking out, I am. "Oh, baby. Everything is going to be all right. I'm here. Thomas is here. Brownie is here."

She clutches the collar of my shirt at the dog's name, and I add, "He's going to be okay, you know. He was hurt. Thomas and I wanted to help him, and that's why we left so early this morning. So he would be safe."

Lexie leans back then, looking at me with tear-filled eyes, and my heart nearly cracks with compassion. "We'll take it one day at a time, okay? It will take a bit for both of us to adjust, but everything is going to be all right."

She lays her head on my shoulder then, sniffing, but I feel her relax a little. I hug her tight, kiss her hair and pray that I am doing the right thing.

♪

WHILE LEXIE AND I take showers, Thomas runs to the grocery store to get food for our dinner and something for Brownie.

Lexie and I are in the kitchen when he comes back, carrying five plastic grocery bags in each hand. He sets them on the table, saying, "I wasn't sure what to get so I just got a lot."

I smile and say, "Something in there smells good."

"They had fresh-baked bread. And I got chicken for Brownie. I thought he might need a little encouragement to eat."

"Want me to fix it for him?"

"Sure. I could find something on TV that Lexie might like while we get everything ready."

"Okay," I say, pulling the container of chicken from the bag.

"There are bowls in the cabinet there," he says, and then to Lexie, "Do you like The Flintstones, or is that too old school?"

I can't help but smile, listening while Thomas wheels Lexie out of the kitchen and offers up multiple selling points on why today's cartoons don't measure up to Pebbles and Bamm-Bamm.

Brownie is awake when I take the bowl of chicken in his room. I sit down on the blanket next to him, rubbing his head and then offering him a bite. He raises up, sniffs it, and then gives it a tentative lick.

"That's it," I say. "Just try a little."

He does, but it's as if he's doing it for me rather than out of any real desire to eat.

Thomas appears in the doorway. "I'd be surprised if he has an appetite any time soon. I just thought we should try."

I nod. "He ate a little."

"We can leave it for him. He might try some more in a while."

"Maybe we should take him outside and see if he can go to the bathroom?"

Thomas squats down to pick him up, carrying him through the back door off the kitchen and into the huge green yard.

He puts Brownie on the grass, supporting him while he tries to stand. He wobbles and starts to fall, but Thomas puts an arm on either side of him, and he is able to pee a little.

"That has to feel better," Thomas says, rubbing the underside of Brownie's neck.

Brownie wags his tail slightly, and I feel tears start in my eyes with the realization that if this new life feels strange to Lexie and me, it will certainly be a whole new existence for Brownie.

"Thank you again, Thomas. For what you've done for him."

"I want him to be okay too."

"I know."

"I'll ask CeCe for the name of her vet. We'll get him checked out there in a day or so."

"Can I ask you something?"

"Of course," he says.

"What will they think about this? About me and Lexie being in your life this way?"

"If they know it's what I want, they'll be happy for me."

"Are you sure about that?" I ask, trying to put myself in their position. "Is there a chance they'll think I'm after your money or something? I mean it has to be a surprise for you to come home with us. It's not exactly the life you're used to leading."

"No, it's not," he admits. "Or it hasn't been, anyway. Don't worry. They're going to love all of you."

We help Brownie back inside then, and I say nothing else of my concern.

♪

Thomas

Point of Expectation

MAYBE WHAT I SHOULD have said is that CeCe will be happy about the sudden changes in my life.

I know Holden and his penchant for thinking I move too fast. It's after midnight when my cell phone rings, and we get into pretty much exactly that.

"You're home? In Nashville? And they're with you?" he asks, sounding more than a little surprised.

"Yeah," I say. "We had kind of an unexpected need to get out of town fast."

"Should I ask?"

"It involved a dog."

"Um, go ahead."

I tell him then about Lila's neighbor and how he kept Brownie chained up all the time. About the dog fight, the shooting and the life-saving veterinarian.

"You're not making this up?" Holden says, incredulous.

"Not a word of it."

"Whoa," Holden says, and then, "Is this permanent? You and Lila?"

I start to answer but realize I have no idea how to do that. "I think we're going to take it one day at a time, Holden. Beyond that, I really don't know."

"Should you get them a place of their own? It seems like a lot to go from no involvement in each other's lives to full-time—"

"I want to know Lexie. I want to be in her life."

"I get that, man. You've just kind of got the pedal to the floor, you know?"

"We didn't exactly plan any of this happening the way it has. Look,

I want you to meet them. Can y'all come over for dinner tomorrow night?"

"Yeah. Sure. And we need to get in the studio later this week. We probably need to have a serious talk sometime before then."

"And you're going to leave it at that?" I say.

"Look, Thomas, I know you just got home, and it sounds like you could use some sleep."

"What's up, Holden? I'd rather hear it now than go to bed wondering."

He sighs, and then says, "The label's not too happy with the sales on our last record."

"What? Since when?"

"Since the president called me two days ago."

"And you're just now telling me this?"

"You weren't here, and I didn't want to add it to everything you already had going on."

"Holden, you don't need to protect me from the hard stuff."

"I wasn't."

"So what are they asking us to do? More touring? What?"

"There's a clause in our contract that basically says the label can opt out if sales are below point of expectation. I believe that's how they put it."

"And sales were below—"

"Point of expectation," Holden finishes.

"Shit," I say.

"Exactly."

"Is there anything we can do?"

"Our tours have been as successful as ever. I think people are just buying and listening to music now in very different ways than they were even three years ago."

"I know I am," I agree.

"I'm just not sure the label is set up to monetize those new ways of listening."

"And if they're not making money, we're not making money."

"Nope."

We sit for a few moments, silence heavy between us. "So let's say they do end the contract," I finally say. "What if we go indy?"

"You read my mind, brother," Holden says.

"I mean what are they doing that we can't really do ourselves? We already have a fan base."

"And the means of reaching them. Right about now, I'm glad CeCe was smart enough to ignore both of us when we said, 'What point is there in building an email list?'"

"The girl is definitely the brains in the trio," I say, actually laughing a little.

"We don't know what's going to happen yet, but we have options. I feel good about that."

"Hey, we've started from scratch before," I agree.

"Yeah."

"Be here at six tomorrow night?"

"We'll be there. Bring the dogs?"

"Sure. Brownie might not be up to meeting them yet, but Lila and Lexie will be."

"Hey, Thomas, I didn't mean to sound like I'm questioning your decision to do the right thing by them. You know I've always got your back."

"I know. It's going to be good, man. Really good."

"CeCe can't wait to meet her."

"They have a lot in common, those two."

"We'll see you tomorrow night. Oh, and Thomas?"

"Yeah?"

"I'm glad you're back. Nashville's actually kind of boring when you're not here."

"You mean you took your eyes off CeCe long enough to notice?"

"That sounds like jealousy."

"Dude—"

Holden laughs then and hangs up.

♪

Lila

No Regrets

THE ROOM IS dark when I wake up. I squint around the room for an alarm clock, spot the digital 9:05 and vault off the bed.

I half-run, half-stumble into Lexie's room, worried that she's been awake, waiting for me. But she's still fast asleep, her sweet face nestled into the soft pillow.

I tiptoe back into the bathroom that connects our rooms, close the door and look at myself in the mirror. My hair is sticking out and up. My eyes are red and puffy. I decide to take a quick shower before allowing Thomas to see me. Ten minutes later, I have to admit I look a little better when I rub away the mirror's condensation and give myself another perusal.

I grab some jeans and a T-shirt from my suitcase and quickly slip them on. My hair is still wet when I leave the room and walk quietly through the house and into the kitchen.

Thomas is sitting at the table with his MacBook and phone in front of him. When he sees me, he slides his chair back and says, "Good morning. How did you sleep?"

"Like a log, apparently," I say, suddenly self-conscious under his scrutiny.

"Coffee?"

"I'd love some."

He goes over to the stove, turns on a kettle of water and then spoons some coffee into a silver pot. "You like it strong?" he asks.

"I do," I say.

The water is boiling within seconds, and he lifts the kettle and fills the pot. He brings it to the table, along with another cup and places it all in front of an empty chair.

"Thank you," I say, sitting down. "What are you doing?"

"I called a couple of friends and asked about schools. There are two within a few miles of here that sound pretty great. What do you think about looking at them today?"

"You don't waste time, do you?" I ask.

He looks unsure how to take my question, and I realize how peevish it sounded. "I'm sorry. I didn't mean anything by that, Thomas. I'm just not used to having anyone do things like this for me."

"It's all right. And I don't want to overstep my boundaries, but I thought you'd want to get a school situation lined up pretty quickly."

"Of course. It's just . . . I guess this has all happened so fast."

He's quiet for a moment, and then, "Are you regretting coming?"

I shake my head. "No, it's not that. I've just been on my own a long time."

"I know it feels different, but isn't it just a little bit of a relief not to carry all of the responsibility yourself?"

"If I'm honest, yes. But somehow, I feel guilty too."

"Why?"

"Because taking care of my daughter shouldn't feel like a burden that's too heavy to carry alone."

"Lila . . . you've done an incredible job with Lexie. And if I hadn't shown up in your life again, you would have continued to do so. I know that. But it's okay for you to still have dreams. To want to achieve some of them. Think maybe that's what you're really feeling guilty about?"

I look at him and shake my head a little. "You're pretty good at reading people."

He shrugs. "Maybe it's more a matter of being able to put yourself in someone else's position for a minute. I think I would feel the same way if I were you."

"Would you?" I ask.

"Yeah. But don't you think Lexie would want you to do the things that make you happy?"

"I do."

"I do too."

I take a sip of my coffee and keep my gaze just short of his. "So tell me about the schools."

♪

Thomas

The One

WE SPEND A few hours that afternoon visiting the two schools that were recommended to me. They were both amazing, clearly set up to provide for Lexie's needs in ways that will be specific to her.

But it is the second school, and a teacher named Mrs. Hamilton, that makes the choice for us. Her instant rapport with Lexie is obvious, and Lexie is immediately taken with her.

We spend nearly an hour in the principal's office, filling out papers and providing the counselor with as much information about Lexie's history as Lila can give her. Once we're done, Mrs. Hamilton comes back into the office and tells us that since this is Friday, Lexie can start on Monday.

She takes Lexie's hand and squeezes it with already notable affection. "We can't wait to see you, Lexie. We're going to have so much fun together."

Lexie's smile is immediate.

Lila is quiet on the walk back to the truck. Once we're on the way to the house, I look at her and say, "Are you sure that's the one?"

She nods, looking out the window. "It's perfect."

"Why does that sound more like a criticism than a compliment?"

"I'm sorry," she says, shaking her head. "I didn't mean it like that."

"What's wrong, Lila?"

"I don't know. It's just that walking through that school, I saw all the things I've been depriving her of."

"Hey," I say, reaching out to take her hand. "That couldn't be any further from the truth. Anything that school has to offer her is secondary to the love and care she's gotten from you."

She looks at me then, tears welling in her eyes. "You think so?"

"I know so."

"Thank you, Thomas."

"I'm the one who should be thanking you."

We drive the rest of the way back to the house without saying anything else. But I don't let go of her hand.

♪

Lila

The Meet

I'M SO NERVOUS that I feel sick. And I have no idea what to wear.

I flip through the few items I took out of my suitcase and hung in this gigantic closet. There's not too much to choose from.

I finally slip a tangerine-colored dress from its hanger and hope it's casual enough, but not too casual.

It's not like I haven't known that CeCe MacKenzie and Holden Ashford were a part of Thomas's life. His best friends. But my awareness of it felt compartmentalized, like something that would never affect me. Almost like he was two people with two different lives.

But that's not true, and the thought of meeting them face to face is terrifying. I force myself to think of other things while I finish getting ready, but am only mildly successful.

I walk into Lexie's room and smile at the picture she makes sitting in the middle of the queen-size bed, propped up against a collection of pillows. She is looking at one of the books Thomas bought for her this afternoon at a small bookshop near the last school we visited.

"Is it good?" I ask.

She looks up at me and smiles, and I am relieved to see that some of her anxiety from the morning seems to have lessened. I had helped her shower and dress before my own shower, so she is ready, her blonde hair in pigtails, her pink cotton dress so perfect for her pale skin.

"We're going to meet some friends of Thomas's tonight," I tell her, moving her chair close to the bed and helping her into it. "They have dogs."

She looks up at me then and smiles again. For Lexie, and maybe me as well, there's no greater seal of approval for a person than the fact that they love dogs.

My hands are shaking as I wheel her from the bedroom and into the hallway. I grasp the chair handles tightly to keep them steady, all the while wishing I could find a reason not to meet them tonight.

We head for the kitchen, and I hear voices just before we reach the doorway. They're already here. I stop, frozen with so many different feelings of dread, inadequacy, and intimidation that I don't think I can make myself move.

"Is that you, Lila?" Thomas calls out, and then I have no choice but to keep going.

I roll the chair through the doorway and onto the kitchen's marble floor. The room is suddenly so quiet that I can hear myself breathing.

Thomas slides off the barstool he's sitting on and walks to us. He stands beside me, leaning over to give Lexie a kiss and tell her how pretty she looks.

And then he turns to face his friends again, saying, "CeCe, Holden, I'd like for you to meet Lila Bellamy and our daughter Lexie."

I do let myself look at them then, surprised to find their expressions welcoming in a way I never expected them to be.

CeCe walks toward us, reaches out to shake my hand. "Hi, Lila. What a pleasure it is to meet you."

"Thank you," I say. "I can't tell you how much I admire your work. It's really so nice to meet you."

"Thank you," she says, and I'm pretty sure I've never seen anyone prettier in real life. Her long hair is thick and glossy; her skin smooth and perfect.

She leans over then to take Lexie's hand and shake it as well, her eyes lit with admiration for my child. And if I hadn't already felt myself falling for her, I guess that would have clinched it.

While CeCe makes small talk with Lexie, Holden walks up, looking from Thomas to me, before saying, "Well, I guess I understand now what all the fuss has been about. Welcome to Nashville, Lila." He leans in then and gives me a hug. He smells like expensive cologne, and there's no wonder why the women at their concerts go crazy over him.

"Thank you, Holden," I say. "I'm still having trouble believing we're really here."

Thomas pushes Lexie farther into the kitchen and says, "I know

Lexie would like to meet Hank Junior and Patsy. Want to let them in from the yard, Holden?"

"Sure," he says, walking to the door and pulling it open.

In trots a huge Walker hound. Scurrying behind is an older, smaller dog wearing a beautiful jeweled collar that jangles.

Lexie's face lights up as if she has been injected with sunshine. Her smile directs them right to her. The hound wags his tail so hard it thumps her chair like a drumbeat. The little dog reaches up to lick Lexie's hand.

Thomas kneels beside her chair and says, "This big guy here is Hank Junior. And this is his sidekick Patsy."

Lexie's giggle melts every heart between us. Hank Junior rests his chin on her knee, and Lexie rubs his ear with the back of her hand, ooohing at its softness.

Lexie and the two dogs don't take their eyes off one another for the next several minutes, while the four of us make small talk.

Thomas and Holden take Lexie outside with them to start the grill, the dogs following them with wagging tails. CeCe and I work on making iced tea in the kitchen.

"I can't believe you're really here," CeCe says, running water into the kettle under the faucet. "Thomas with a woman in his house who's not temporary. I mean . . . wait, that sounded so—"

"True?" I say with a half-smile.

"Inappropriate," she says, sheepish.

"Honesty is a good thing."

"So is diplomacy. It's just that Thomas hasn't had any one particular girl in his life."

"I kind of guessed that," I say. "If it weren't for Lexie, I'm sure I wouldn't be here."

CeCe looks as if she might disagree just to make me feel better, but stops short of it, shaking her head. "Whatever the reason, I'm glad you're both here. He's needed a change in his life."

"What do you mean?"

"This existence can get a little out of control if you let it. Women throwing themselves at him nearly everywhere he goes. There aren't too many guys who can handle that without messing up from time to time. At least for Holden, I'm something of a barrier. Although, you'd be surprised what some women will do when they set their sights on a guy."

"Got any good examples?" I ask, smiling a little.

"A bunch," CeCe says, opening tea bags as she talks. "When we were doing a show in New York City, two girls hid in a dumpster outside the stadium entrance we were planning to go in through. Bless their hearts, by the time they jumped out at Holden and Thomas, they smelled just awful!"

I laugh. I can't help it. "Those are definitely some desperate measures."

"I did appreciate their determination," CeCe says, shaking her head. "I let them have a couple of my outfits, and we put them in front-row seats. You've got to appreciate someone who will go to those lengths to support your work. Even if it is because they think you have a hot body."

I laugh. "That was really nice of you. I imagine there are a lot of celebrities who would have had them hauled off by security."

She tips her head side to side. "My theory is you have to remember who put you where you are."

"Not everyone thinks that way."

"I guess not. I heard about this pop star who was supposed to meet some girls who had won a contest. Apparently, she blew them off big time, and the mom wrote a blog post about what a horrible experience it was. Not the kind of publicity you want, that's for sure."

"Do you like being famous?" I ask, opening the ice-maker and filling a bowl.

CeCe shrugs. "I like having achieved a lot of the things I've dreamed about achieving. I guess there are all different levels of famous. Ours is a much quieter version than some, and I don't think I would enjoy it being too much more than it is. Crazy things can happen when people start to think you're not a real person."

"Like the shooting in DC," I say.

She nods. "It's hard to believe that people can get that far out in their thinking, but it happens."

"I'm so sorry for what you all went through," I say. "I can't imagine."

"It was rough," CeCe says. "I don't think we'll ever completely get past it."

"I understand," I say, picking up a towel to dry my hands.

CeCe looks at me for a moment, and then says, "Have you had something like that—"

"Sort of," I say softly. I hesitate, but feel prompted to be honest with her. "My father killed my mother when I was a senior in high school."

"Oh, Lila. Oh, my gosh. I'm so sorry."

I glance at her face, see how deeply my words have affected her. "I really don't know why I just told you that. I never talk about it."

She reaches out and squeezes my arm. "Maybe you just recognized someone who would understand where you've been. I do."

"These aren't things you ever get over. You just live through them and find a way to go on with a great big hole in your heart."

CeCe nods. "Is your father—"

"He's in prison, actually. On death row."

"Lila, I'm so sorry."

I shake my head. "It's not something I can change. More than anything, I wish I could, but we can only be responsible for our own actions. Not other people's."

CeCe studies me for several seconds, as if she's weighing what to say. I realize how uncomfortable I must have made her. "Look, this is a dreary way to start a friendship," I say. "Or what I hope will be a friendship."

"I think I have to disagree. We've started with honesty. That's a far better place to start than the superficial stuff people usually lead with."

I consider what she's said and then, "Do you have a lot of friends here?"

"Holden and Thomas are my BFF's. We just all get one another in ways I can't even explain. I like meeting new people, but I have to say, this industry puts a different spin on opening yourself up to someone you don't know very well. I've had quotes show up on websites that were nothing like what I actually said during a conversation."

"That has to be frustrating."

"You learn to edit yourself and limit what you say. Which makes letting someone get to know you a pretty tricky thing."

"That would take some getting used to."

The tea kettle starts to whistle, and CeCe picks it up and pours the water into a stone pitcher, then adds the tea bags. "May I ask you something?"

I nod. "Sure."

"Did you ever think about contacting Thomas and letting him know about Lexie?"

"Only a thousand times," I say.

"Why didn't you?" she asks. There's no judgement in the question, just an obvious desire to know.

"I didn't want to be one of those girls who expect a guy to sign over his life just because they spent one night together."

"But he was just as responsible as you—"

"I know. And I think I knew he would have done whatever he could. I just didn't want to have him that way, you know?"

"Can I ask what's different now?"

"I see how much he wants to be in Lexie's life. Whether he and I are ever anything else beyond being her parents, he's convinced me he wants to be in her life, and I know he has a right to that."

"He looks so happy," CeCe says. "I haven't seen him look the way he looks tonight in a long time."

I shake my head and laugh a little. "I don't think it's because I've made his life simple the past several days."

"I don't think Thomas needs simple," CeCe says. "I think he needs real."

"You can't get much more real than stealing a dog from a dog fight and skipping town to keep from getting caught."

"My hero!" CeCe exclaims, her eyes going wide. "Tell me more."

I tell her about Rowdy, how he had been my landlord, how he called Brownie "Killer" and kept him on a chain every day of his life. "And the night before we left to come here, he decided to put him in a dog fight. We saw him leave with Brownie in the truck, and I knew it had to be something bad because he never took him anywhere. So Thomas and I followed him. By the time we were able to get to Brownie, he was in really bad shape."

"And you have him here?"

I nod. "Would you like to see him?"

"Yes!" she says, her whole face lighting up.

I lead the way to the small room where Brownie has been staying. He's asleep when we step in, but he opens his eyes after a few seconds and looks up at me. His tail starts to thump on his comfy bed.

I squat down next to him and begin rubbing his head. "CeCe, this is Brownie. Brownie, meet CeCe."

"Oh, my goodness," CeCe says, her gaze moving from Brownie's sweet face to the wounds evident across his body. Tears well in her eyes, and she instantly starts to cry. She drops onto her knees next to me and lets him sniff the back of her hand before she rubs under his neck. He thumps his tail again, and I can see on CeCe's face her understanding of his pain and everything he's been through.

I fully believe that a lot of times you don't have to have a lot of details to know everything you need to know about a person. There are a few key things that paint a perfect picture of who they are. I think about the things CeCe and I are likely to have in common: a love for music and singing, a role in Thomas's life. But I think this piece of her, her instant empathy for this poor dog who's known so little joy in his life is what will make me, time and again, so happy to know her.

♪

Thomas

One Day at a Time

WHEN WE SIT DOWN to eat, it's already eight o'clock, and we're all starving. Luckily, Holden's grill skills are better than mine, and the food smells wonderful.

Lila and I do a good job of avoiding eye contact for most of the night. It's as if we don't know how to act around each other now that CeCe and Holden are part of the picture. I wish I could push a fast-forward button and just get to the part where it doesn't feel weird because we all know one another.

Lexie is so tired she can barely hold her eyes open. I help her eat. And throughout the entire meal, I feel Holden and CeCe looking at me as if I am some nearly unrecognizable version of myself. Which, I guess from their point of view, I am.

I don't mind though. I actually like the way it feels to help my daughter, to hear her laugh when I say something she thinks is funny.

It's different from anything I've ever felt in my life. I feel love for her, but it's unique from all the other love I've known. It's like every time I let my eyes settle on her, the feeling intensifies. I want to protect her, help her, step in front of whatever speeding cars might come her way in this life.

And I guess that shows on my face because when Lila takes Lexie to her room to tuck her in, both Holden and CeCe say at the same time, "What did you do with him?"

I shake my head and laugh, leaning back in my chair, hands behind my head. "Sure you want him back?"

"I like this Thomas," CeCe says, smiling. "You're head over heels. Who knew you had this daddy side?"

"Not me," I concede.

"So how does this go?" Holden asks. "Are you and Lila—"

"Right now, we're just playing it by ear," I say. "The one-day-at-a-time thing."

"Do you have feelings for Lila, Thomas?" CeCe asks in her pull-no-punches manner.

"Did you see her?" Holden asks, grinning. "I know he's got some kind of feelings for her."

CeCe play-slaps him, and then looks at me. "She seems kind of vulnerable."

"Yeah," I say, serious now. "She's had some tough stuff in her life."

"We talked some. She told me a little. She just seems like someone you could really hurt."

I hear the protective note in CeCe's voice and realize she's already seeing in Lila what I see in her. "That's the last thing I want to do," I say.

"Your track record's not so great, dude," Holden says.

"You're one to talk," I say, and then feeling CeCe giving us both a visual dressing down, I add, "I mean before CeCe, of course."

"Of course," she says, shaking her head and rolling her eyes.

"I don't really know of any other way to do this than taking it one day at a time," I say, serious now. "I'm pretty sure I'm going to make some mistakes. I've never been a father, and you both know I've played the field and then some."

"Do you care about her?" CeCe asks. "Lila, I mean."

"Aw, come on now. How could he know for sure?" Holden asks. "They've spent a few days together after not seeing each other for nine years, and before that, it was one night."

CeCe throws him a searing look and says, "Thomas, we're not trying to stick our noses where they don't belong. But you know we have a little habit of watching out for you."

Holden temples his fingers the way he does when he's trying to be quiet and having trouble doing so.

"Well, one of us does," CeCe adds. "And one of us might be just a little jealous."

"Hey," Holden says.

"You know it's true," CeCe says. "You're like a mother hen when it comes to protecting Thomas from the fairer sex."

Holden rolls his eyes. "Yeah, like he needs protecting."

Hank Junior walks over and puts his chin on my leg, looking up at me with imploring eyes. I pass him one of the french fries on my plate, knowing CeCe's going to scold me. And she does.

"One french fry won't hurt him," I say. And then Patsy gets up from her spot on the floor and dawdles over and gives me a 'pretty-please' look.

"Now you're going to corrupt both of them," Holden says.

"Y'all need to let these two live a little. What fun is life if you have to be on a diet all the time?"

"The only diet these two are on," Holden says, "is a see-food diet."

CeCe smiles and shakes her head. "That's because you're such a pushover. Both of you."

Lila appears in the doorway then. She looks at me with an uncertain smile, and it occurs to me, for the first time, how it might feel to be her with the three of us. Feeling like an outsider.

I stand and pull out a chair for her. She looks shy as she walks over and sits down next to me.

"Did she go to sleep?" I ask.

"I think as soon as her head hit the pillow," Lila says.

Holden leans forward on the table, looking at Lila. "Thomas says you have quite a voice."

"That probably depends on who you compare me to," she says, not quite meeting Holden's gaze.

"Do you have anything recorded?" CeCe asks. "Just something we could hear."

"Nothing that's very high quality," Lila answers.

"I thought we could help her get some demo work," I say, looking at CeCe. "That's always a good place to get your sea legs."

"It was for me," CeCe agrees. "I'd be happy to make some calls in the morning.

Lila looks at her, clearly grateful. "That's really nice," she says. "But, please, don't feel like—"

"I don't," CeCe interrupts. "I want to."

"But you haven't even heard me sing," Lila starts.

"If Thomas says you're that good," CeCe says, "that's all I need to know."

It's no secret that I think CeCe pretty much hung the moon. But every now and then, she reminds me, in the biggest kind of way, why I think Holden is such a damn lucky guy.

♪

Lila

A Part of Things

CECE AND HOLDEN have already gone, and Thomas and I are in the kitchen, putting away the last few things from the dishwasher.

"Thank you, Thomas," I say, focusing on wiping away a few drips of water from a bowl so I don't have to look at him.

"For what?" he asks.

"For making me feel like such a part of things," I say.

"I very much want you to be a part of things."

"All three of you are almost too good to be true though."

"You've only seen us at our best. Don't let us fool you. We can get some serious arguments going every now and then."

"I find that hard to believe," I say, shaking my head.

"Hang around long enough, and—" He stops there, as if regretting his choice of words. "That's what I want you to do, you know."

"What?"

"Hang around."

"This feels like a dream," I say.

"There's opportunity here, Lila. And you've got talent. We both know that. You also know how to work hard. You put those two things together, and your dreams really can come true."

"I feel a little bit like I'm cutting in line. CeCe calling people for me and—"

"Hey, you use what you've got. Everybody does. This whole town, this industry is based on relationships. That's true for every level on the ladder. CeCe might get you in with a producer, but you'll have to do the work that keeps you there. Prove yourself. Impress them."

"I don't know if I can do that though."

"I know you can."

He steps closer and takes the towel out of my hand. He hooks one

45

arm around my waist, looking down at me. And I look up at him. I really could let myself completely drown in his eyes. I guess he must read my thoughts because he lowers his head and kisses me with the softest touch, and then deeply, a full, ripe kiss that makes no secret of the mutual attraction between us.

I slide my arms around his neck and link my hands together. I want to hold on, to just stay here, right here in this circle of pleasure and comfort and safety. To press myself against him in complete awareness of what it is I'm asking for.

I let myself do that for a couple of minutes, until our kissing has caught fire, blazing outward and upward until we both become aware that we are igniting something that is almost beyond our ability to reel in.

I force myself to step back, wiping my hand over my mouth and drawing in a quick breath. "Thomas—"

"I know," he says, raking his hands through his hair. "I'm sorry. I—"

"No. Don't be. I'm not sorry. I'm just . . . I have to be smarter than this."

"Lila—"

I hold up a hand and stop him. "We should check on Brownie. Take him outside before bedtime. And we need to give him his antibiotic too."

I watch as Thomas forces in a chest full of air and then slowly releases it back out. "Yeah," he says. "We do need to do that. And then get a good night's sleep."

"A good night's sleep," I say. "Right."

♪

Thomas

Sleepless

IT'S TWO O'CLOCK when I hear the text message ding on my phone.

Since I couldn't be any more awake, I roll over and grab it, squinting at the screen.

Hey.

It's Carrie Summerfield, a girl I met after a concert a month or so ago. I should ignore the text, but she's nice, and I'm awake.

Hey.

You're not sleeping either.

No.

Why not?

Good question.

Um, I could come over. Keep you up even later.

I hesitate over the screen. Not that long ago, I would have taken her up on it. I let myself consider whether it bothers me that I can't do that tonight. I think about Lila, asleep downstairs, about kissing her in the kitchen earlier. About how I'd wanted to do a lot more than kiss her.

I tap the screen and type my response.

Gonna renew my effort here. Early day tomorrow.

Sure?

Yeah. Goodnight.

Night. ?

♪

Lila

No Easy Time to Go

TURNS OUT THERE'S a lot that's awkward about two people enrolling their child in school and accompanying her on the first day.

Most of the teachers assumed, and not that I can blame them, that Thomas and I are married. After the second time of correcting the impression, we both just let it be.

We've been in Nashville three days now, and I still very much feel like a fish out of water. And not because of anything Thomas has done. He's done pretty much everything a person could do to make both Lexie and me as comfortable as possible.

We went shopping for school clothes for Lexie, and items the school had recommended she would need for her classes. Thomas had insisted as well that we buy some things for me.

The stores we went to were as different from anything I'm used to as they could be. Small, boutique-type stores that specialize in specific looks and items. In every place, Thomas was recognized, of course.

He's always gracious about it, stopping to sign autographs and chat for a minute with whoever it is complimenting his music. Like CeCe, he sees it as part of what he does and has an attitude of appreciation for the people who support his work.

At the same time, I can see how going out in public would become something you'd rather avoid doing simply because it would become about so much more than just running an errand.

Thomas definitely has a way with people though, and we didn't leave one fan feeling like they had been shorted by him.

In one of the shops, the sales girl had been so excited to help me pick out a couple of dresses. Thomas had taken Lexie outside to keep her entertained while I tried on a few things. The girl smiled a conspiratorial smile at me and said, "So what look does he like for you? Smart and hot? Just smart? Country hot?"

She laughs a little, but I can tell she has every intention of making sure Thomas is as happy with our picks as I am. I can't blame her. It's probably not every day that she gets to directly help a full-blown country music star.

Even so, I was pretty firm about letting her know when something didn't suit me.

I'm wearing one of the dresses today. It's kind of this sea blue green, sleeveless with three white buttons down the front. I've never worn anything that made me feel as pretty as this dress. As much as I love it, I feel incredibly guilty about the price tag. After realizing how much it cost, I hadn't wanted to get it, but Thomas insisted. And even though I told myself I would pay him back eventually for the clothes, I can only imagine how long it will take me to earn that much extra money.

The look on his face this morning when I walked into the kitchen was almost worth the guilt.

"I just love your dress," Miss Tipton, Lexie's math teacher, says to me, glancing the length of it with notable envy.

"Thank you," I say, dropping my gaze when Thomas looks at me and smiles.

Miss Tipton turns her attention to something her teacher's aide is asking her.

Thomas leans in close to my ear and says, "See. I told you it was worth it."

The feel of his warm breath against my skin sends a shiver through me which I quickly try to blink away. "You don't mind not playing fair, do you?"

"Not at all," he says. "As long as I get my way."

Miss Tipton turns her attention back to us then, and we continue the conversation on what Lexie will be covering in her class and how we might help her at home. When we finish meeting with each of her teachers, it's time to leave Lexie there for the remainder of the day.

My throat starts to feel tight in the way it always does when I leave Lexie somewhere new. I watch her closely to see if she's going to be sad when we go, but her attention is already focused on a little girl who is showing her a drawing. Lexie points at something in the center of the paper and smiles at her. The little girl smiles back at her.

"This might be the easiest time for you to go," Miss Tipton says, a look of understanding on her face.

I nod once, but the tears well up despite my resolve not to let Lexie see them. I lean in and give her a quick kiss on the head and walk out of the room. My footsteps echo on the school's tile hallway.

I head straight for the main door and don't stop until I'm standing outside next to Thomas's truck. I fold my arms across my chest in the way I have a habit of doing when I feel like I'm about to fall apart over something.

I hear Thomas's footsteps behind me and then I feel his hand on my shoulder. He turns me toward him and pulls me into his arms in a loose hug, as if he's not sure I will welcome the embrace.

But I do. Because I'm not used to having someone help me hold myself together.

"Damn," he says. "That was hard."

The tears slide down my face then, and there's nothing I can do to stop them. "I hate leaving her," I say.

"We could always homeschool."

"I've thought about it so many times, but there's something about being around other kids that is obviously so good for her. She handles this far better than I do."

"Better than me too," he agrees.

I pull back and let myself look up into his uneasy gaze.

"You've done this so many times, haven't you?" he says.

"I'd like to tell you it gets easier," I say. "But it really doesn't."

"Yeah."

We get in the truck, silent now as we pull out of the parking lot. I think about some of the other times I left her in daycare or the nursery at church, or school, and I remember how lonely those times had felt because it was just me, handling all of those feelings alone. Painful as it is this morning, I realize it's really nice to have someone who cares about her in the way I do to share these moments with.

I have an overwhelming urge to reach across and take his hand in mine. But that feels somehow almost like it would be asking for too much in light of everything he's already given us. So I lace my fingers tightly together and keep my hands where they are. And let it be enough.

♪

Thomas

Hard and Fast

IN THE AFTERNOON, I meet Holden at his house for a writing session. Lila comes with me, and then leaves with CeCe a few minutes after we get there. CeCe had offered to drive her around to meet a few of the producers she had called about demo work for Lila. As excited as I could tell Lila was, I also sensed her terror. But then if anyone could put her at ease, it would be CeCe.

Sometime last year, Holden had completed the studio at one end of the house he and CeCe built together. It's not huge, but it's more than everything we need. I actually love the privacy of it and how it feels like we can be who we used to be before anyone had a clue who we were.

He can write dumb lines, and I can sing off-key. Neither one of us minds a bit. In fact, I'd say having the freedom to do that is how we've gotten some of our best work on the page.

This afternoon proves to be no exception. Holden has written several dumb lines, and I've been off-key more times than I care to admit.

"What's going on?" Holden asks, tossing his notebook on the desk and leaning back in his chair.

"What do you mean?"

"You're clearly preoccupied."

"I guess," I say.

"Everything all right?"

"We took Lexie to school this morning for her first day."

"How'd it go?" Holden asks, a note of compassion in his voice.

"Ah, it pretty much sucked."

"Man, you've fallen hard and fast, haven't you?"

I shake my head and say, "Everybody tells you what it's like to be a parent, to know you've been part of bringing a child into the world.

But it's like so many other things, I guess. You just have no way of knowing until you've held that child in your arms and realized how much you're going to care about what happens to her and how the world treats her."

Holden considers what I've said, and then half-smiling, says, "Who are you? And what have you done with Thomas Franklin?"

I laugh a little. "Yeah, I realize I'm becoming unrecognizable."

"I wouldn't say that. I might envy you just a little bit."

"What? You ready for children?"

Holden shrugs. "Yeah. I think so."

"And CeCe isn't?"

"She hasn't said that."

"Nothing wrong with being ready."

"Not that you're the poster boy for that particular choice."

"That, I am not," I say. "Then again, if I had to sit around trying to figure out if I was ready or not, this probably isn't a choice I would ever have ended up making."

"I'm gonna agree with you on that one." Holden picks up his guitar, strums a few chords and hums a bit before adding the lines:

baby girl, baby girl
who knew you'd change my whole world

And we go from there. Because that's how it's always been with Holden and me. Once we understand where the other one is, what the other one is thinking about, we kind of have a way of synching up, moving forward from the same page. If I had to say what I value most about our friendship, it would be that.

As much as we joke and give each other crap, no one has ever been able to read me better and write things for me to sing about that are actually part of who I am.

No way to put a value on that.

♪

Lila

Last Word on the Last Note

CECE HAS THE top down on her white Porsche Carrera, and we roll through the streets of Music Row with the radio just loud enough that we can still talk.

CeCe waves at nearly every other car, and it's clear that she does not subscribe to the big-hat, dark sunglasses way of dealing with celebrity.

"You don't mind being recognized so much?" I ask.

"I guess when you ask for something, you kind of need to own the results."

"Does it ever get old?"

"Maybe when I try to run into Whole Foods without a stitch of makeup on, and I see my picture in some magazine looking like death warmed over."

I laugh. I can't help it. "You could never look like that."

"Oh, don't go there."

I smile at that and then say, "I can't tell you how much I appreciate your doing this for me, CeCe. It really is an awful lot of trouble for you to go to."

"It really isn't," she says. "These are all folks I've known for a long time now. They helped me get my start by giving me work when I needed it. They're good people. I wouldn't hook you up with anyone who was anything short of that."

"Thank you so much. Really."

"You are so welcome."

"I hope they won't feel like they should hire me just because you're—"

"Stop," CeCe says, putting a hand on my arm. "They won't. Believe me. They're all professionals, and they have their products to sell just like the rest of us. Writers who come in to get a song demoed expect a quality performance, and that's what you're gonna give them."

A few minutes later when we pull into the parking lot of the studio, I'm not sure which is thumping harder: my heart or the butterflies in my stomach. I have such an overwhelming fear of failing at this, I can hardly breathe.

My hands are shaking as I get out of the car, the door shutting behind me with a solid-sounding *wachunk*.

CeCe walks around and gives me a reinforcing smile. "You really are going to live through this. In an hour, I'm going to be saying 'I told you so.'"

I say a silent prayer that she will be right because having someone like her go to all this trouble for me is just about more than I can comprehend.

The studio is like something out of a magazine. Sound-proofing panels line the walls. A computer with a massive screen sits on a desk with lots of other technical equipment surrounding it. The producer, Joe Michaels, walks out of the sound booth, smiling at CeCe and pulling her into a warm hug.

"Hey, you," he says. "Long time, no CeCe."

CeCe rolls her eyes and laughs. "I see you haven't lost your corny sense of humor."

"Unfortunately for everyone who has to work with me, no."

He looks at me then, and I do my best to act as if I'm not wilting on the inside when I actually am.

CeCe touches my shoulder and says, "This is Lila Bellamy. Thomas says she sings like an angel. I've yet to have the privilege of hearing her, but—"

"If Thomas says it," Joe allows with a smile, "it must be true."

I want to shake my head and protest, "No, really," because the pressure building up inside me at the thought of having to live up to those words is enough to make me turn and run out of the studio. But I force my feet to stay where they are, plant a smile on my face and say, "Thank you so much, Mr. Michaels."

"Joe. It's Joe. Lila?"

"Yes," I say with a nod.

"Why don't we put you in the sound booth and knock out a track?"

This, I had not expected, although I guess when you're applying for a singing job, it would make sense that they would expect you to sing. "Ah, okay. Anything in particular you'd like me to do?"

"Tell me what you like. I probably have it."

I pick a song I've known since I was a teenager. One where the words are embedded in my memory from having sung it so many times before.

He says, "Great," and sits down at the computer keyboard, searching for a minute or so. "There. Ready when you are."

I glance at CeCe, expecting her to say she'll be back later. But she shows no signs of leaving. While the thought of singing in front of her makes me feel physically ill, I suppose that sooner or later, I'm going to have to if I intend to go after this crazy dream of mine.

"You'll be great," she says.

I turn and walk to the sound booth, step inside and close the door behind me. Joe taps the mike.

I put on the headphones and hear him say, "There's bottled water there beside you. Help yourself."

"Thank you." I reach for one, open the cap and take a sip, probably more as a delaying tactic than out of thirst. But the water soothes the dryness in my throat. I close my eyes and sit for a moment, letting the words from the lyric loop through my mind. When I'm sure that they're all there in place, I look at Joe and nod.

He clicks the track, and the music starts. I close my eyes again because putting myself in another place seems like the best way to kill the nerves inside me. I hit the first verse off the last note of the intro and follow the lyric through the song, letting my mind wander to other times in my life when I sang these words and loved them so much.

Something in that erases all the fear and leaves nothing in its wake, except my love for music and the lyrics and the feelings they inspire.

I don't open my eyes again until I've left the last word on the last note. When I open them, I spot CeCe first. She's standing behind Joe, smiling. I can see in her face that she thinks I nailed it.

Joe leans back in his chair, claps softly. "Whoa. Turns out Thomas was right, huh? I have an opening tomorrow afternoon, Lila, for a writer needing a female vocal. If you want it, it's yours."

And I smile then. Just this smile that starts way down deep inside me and breaks across my face. I can feel the warmth of it spreading through me like sunshine on a June day at the beach. "Thank you," I say, looking at them both. "Thank you so very much."

♪

Thomas

Swimming in the Middle

"YOU KNOW THAT smile looks really good on you."

I look at Thomas from the passenger seat of his truck. I have to admit I can't stop. "I know," I say, shaking my head. "I look like a gloating fool."

"No, that's not it," he says. "You look like a girl who's gotten something she's wanted for a really long time. And that's just cool."

I look down at my hands and try to school my expression into something a little more neutral. "Don't think that I believe for a minute, any of this would have happened without you and CeCe."

"It might not have happened today, but I fully believe it would have happened."

"Why do you believe in me so much?"

"Umm, because I know what it feels like to want this dream, Lila. To love the music so much that you just want to spend your life diving in and swimming in the middle of it as often as you can."

"It really is like that, isn't it?" she says.

"Yeah, it really is."

I park the truck at the front of the school. We take our cue from the other parents waiting in line, staying where we are until a bell rings. Car doors open simultaneously, mostly mothers spilling out, a dad here and there. Lila and I get out of the truck at the same time and walk to the entrance door. Inside, we head for the classroom where we had been told Lexie would have her last subject for the day.

We stand in the doorway until the teacher spots us and waves us inside. I immediately see Lexie in one corner of the room. She's sitting in her chair next to another little girl in a similar chair. They're playing a version of patty-cake and giggling in a way that just untethers whatever remaining guards I've had on my heart. Those guards spool off into oblivion, and I think to myself: *Dear Lord, I love that child. Help me to be everything she needs.*

The teacher, Mrs. Saddler, if I remember correctly, looks at Lila and me both before saying, "What a pleasure it is to have Lexie in this class. She has already added so much to this day. I believe she's made a couple of fast new friends."

"I see that," Lila says, smiling in the direction of Lexie and her playmate.

"I think she'll do very well here," Mrs. Saddler says. "We're so glad you chose us for her school."

She tells us about a couple of things Lexie can practice at home tonight. We thank her again, and then I walk over to help Lexie with her book bag.

Lila leans over and kisses the top of Lexie's head and then speaks to the little girl next to her. And as I wheel the chair from the classroom, I have to wonder how all of this could feel so right, so fast. But then I guess there's really only one answer that makes sense. And that is because it is right.

♪

Lila

A Good Place

I MAKE DINNER that night, spaghetti with a red sauce for Lexie and something a little different for Thomas and me. An olive oil and rosemary dressing I came up with a few years ago that has become one of my favorites.

Lexie is working on a drawing for her art class when we sit down to eat. Thomas compliments her on the colors and the dog, which looks an awful lot like Brownie, he says.

This makes her smile.

"Brownie's feeling a lot better," I tell her. "We even took him for a little walk today."

This makes Lexie smile again. Thomas helps her with her noodles, giving her a bite and then taking a bite of his own.

Certain foods she manages on her own pretty well. Noodles aren't one of them. But he doesn't make any big deal of it, and, in between bites, she continues with her drawing.

Thomas looks at me and says, "I think Holden and I hammered out a pretty good song this morning."

"I'd love to hear it," I say.

"After we get a little more polish on it," Thomas says.

"You can't even tell me what it's about?"

"I think I'll wait. Make it a surprise."

We've just finished eating when my cell phone rings from the living room where I had left it earlier. "Be right back," I say. I see Macy's name is on the screen. I show it to Thomas and say, "Have you got Lexie for a few minutes?"

"Sure," he says.

I answer and walk outside on the terrace at the back of the house, so glad to hear her voice. "It seems like ten years since I've seen you," I say.

"Fifteen from here," she says. "How the heck are you?"

"Good," I say. "Still trying to catch my breath a little. But it's been pretty amazing."

"I like amazing," Macy says. "Tell me."

I do tell her then, about Lexie's school, about CeCe and Holden, about the demo work I'm starting tomorrow. "It all seems like something out of a dream," I say.

"Well, it's not," she says. "And you deserve every moment of it."

"No, I don't know that I deserve any of it."

"Be happy for these changes, hon. You're in a good place. And life here for you was becoming anything but a good place. How's Brownie?"

"He's good. We took him to the vet yesterday, and he's made incredible improvement. He's eating. He'll be getting his stitches out in a week or so."

"That's awesome. I boxed up your things today, and I hope you don't mind, but if there was something I didn't think you were ever going to use or would want, I took it over to the Goodwill."

"Thank you, Macy. That's so beyond the call of duty."

"Oh, I'll be asking for payment. Expect to see me in Nashville soon."

"I cannot wait," I say.

"Do you really mean that?"

"Of course, I mean it. I miss you like crazy. Did you see Rowdy when you were out there?"

"Unfortunately, I did see the crazy loon. Good heavens, what a piece of human waste."

I laugh. I can't help it. "Did he say anything about Brownie?"

Macy hesitates as if she's not sure she should say something she's reluctant to say. "He said you killed his dog, and that if you and Thomas hadn't shown up there that night, everything would have been fine."

"Oh, until the next time he decided to throw him in a fighting ring?"

"Yeah, that," Macy says. "Look, Lila. He's got several bolts loose in that cranium of his. I don't trust him not to do something insane like come and find you or something."

"He wouldn't do that. Not even he is that crazy. I do know that he's been in jail before and that the last thing in the world he wants is to ever go back."

"Well, if you were sane, that might be a deterrent. Since that doesn't apply to him—"

"Don't worry," I say. "Okay? But you don't go anywhere near him again."

"Not planning to," she says. "But seriously, just don't ever let him find out that you have the dog. There was some kind of look in his eyes today . . . I wouldn't put anything past him."

"I won't."

"How's that precious girl of mine?"

"Oh, Macy, I wish you could have seen her at school today. It's just this incredible place that can do things for her that I never imagined being able to give her."

"Then that makes it all worthwhile, doesn't it?"

"Yeah," I say. "I'm so grateful to Thomas for doing this for her. But Macy, oh my gosh, the tuition is over $50,000 a year."

"He's her father, Lila. You know he's stepped up to the plate in a way that so many guys in his position would never have done. I mean, who wouldn't be crazy about that child? Let him do for her what he can do. His part is different from your part, but you are both critical to her. To her happiness and getting all of her needs met. She needs both of you."

I can't deny the truth in the words. I know my best friend is right. I've made do all these years for both of us, but no matter how I look at it, it wasn't enough for Lexie. Or at least, in the end, it wouldn't have been. She needs things I wasn't able to give her. Things that Thomas can give her.

"All right. Don't go glum on me," Macy says. "End of this discussion. Tell me about this demo stuff tomorrow."

I start in about it then, tell her about the studio, Joe Michaels and the song I sang. And how gracious CeCe has been in calling around and talking me up the way she has.

"So she's not all looks, huh?" Macy says.

"No," I agree, "she's not."

"It hardly seems fair that someone could look that good, sound that good and be that nice," Macy grumbles.

"I'll give you that, but she is all of those things."

"You're not gonna boot me out of best friend status, are you?"

I hear a vulnerable note in her voice that I have rarely, if ever, heard. "Hey, of course not. You put the best in friend," I say.

"Oh, my gosh, that's corny," Macy laughs.

I laugh too. "It might be corny, but it's true. You've done more for me than I'll ever be able pay you back for."

"Hey, one trip to Nashville. You fix me up with a cowboy type who sings, and we're even."

"Does this mean Garth is out of the picture?"

"Soooo out of the picture," she says.

"Well, thank goodness for that."

"Believe me, I've already heard it from Mama."

"You know your mama's always right."

"Do you have to rub it in? Speaking of which, I gotta go. I promised her I would go to this supper at church with her tonight."

"Whaat?"

Macy laughs again. "Gotta keep you guessing, don't I?"

"You definitely do," I say. "I love you, Macy."

"Love you, girl. See ya."

♪

Lila

Sweet Tea and Me

THOMAS DRIVES ME to the studio. We get there about ten minutes early.

"Are you sure you don't want me to go with you?" he asks, draping his arms over the steering wheel.

"I'm about to die of nerves as it is," I say. "With you standing out there listening, I don't think I'd have a chance."

"Ah, come on, everybody needs a groupie."

I laugh. "I guess it is nice to have one."

"You're gonna do great," he says. "How late were you up last night going over the song?"

"Not too late," I say.

"You're good with it though?"

"Yeah. I think so."

"Text me when you're done, and I'll swing back to get you."

"You're picking up Lexie, right? Sorry," I say, since we've already talked about it three times.

"Hey, if I never understood the phrase 'overprotective parent,' I now do, believe me."

I slide out of the truck then, look over my shoulder and wave once at him. I force myself to walk through the studio's main doors, one foot in front of the other, isolating my thoughts to nothing beyond each step. No chickening out. No throwing away an opportunity.

Joe and a twenty-something guy are waiting for me when I walk into the room.

"Lila. Hey," Joe says, coming over to shake my hand. He turns to make introductions. "Taylor, this is Lila Bellamy. Lila, Taylor Pendleton. It's his song you'll be singing today. 'Sweet Tea and Me.'"

We shake hands, and I smile with as much appreciation as I dare since I don't want him to think he's getting a complete novice to sing his song. "I really love it," I say. "It's an awesome lyric."

The words clearly mean something to him. I wonder then if maybe he's as inexperienced as I am.

"Thanks," he says. "I really can't wait to hear you sing it. It's one thing to hear me singing it when I'm writing it. Believe me, it's hard to imagine it actually sounding good when I'm all I have to go by."

I laugh then. "I'm sure you're not that bad."

"Ohh, I am. Writer here. Singer. Not here."

"You got the lyrics?" Joe asks.

I pull the paper from my purse. "Yeah."

"All right. Let's get started."

♪

Lila

Wings

THE NEXT FEW weeks take on routine, and a way of life that is at once full and busy, exciting and fulfilling.

Lexie absolutely loves her school. It's all I can do to get her ready quickly enough every morning once she wakes up because she's so anxious to get out the door. A little part of my heart knows this is the beginning of a new independence for her, and the realization for us both that she doesn't need me in the way she once did.

The selfish part of me, the part that wants to keep her to myself forever, and never let her out into the world where I know there will be potential for her to be hurt and challenged, feels sadness at this realization. But the logical part of me, the part that knows Lexie's ability to be as independent as possible will ultimately make her life much more secure and rewarding.

And since those are the things I want most for her, I practice on a daily basis reminding myself that everything happening for her is for the best.

That doesn't make it easy, however.

We've been in Nashville nearly a month when Thomas and I commiserate about this very thing one night when Lexie is already asleep. We're sitting outside on the terrace at the back of the house, sharing some wine he had been wanting to open for a while.

"It's kind of the best and the worst, isn't it?" he says, looking at me with a knowing expression.

"What do you mean?" I ask.

"Giving her wings even when you know you're loosening the roots."

"So I'm not the only one struggling?"

"No, you're not. Although I concede it has to feel a gazillion times harder to you."

"I've never seen her this happy," I say.

"Her teachers can't say enough positive things."

"I'm so proud of her, but I know none of it would be happening if it weren't for you."

"I don't want credit for that, Lila."

"I know you don't, but I'd like to give it to you anyway."

He stares off into the night for a moment before saying, "When you realize that you have a lot of money, you start thinking of all these things that seem like they would make life so much better. At first, it really seems like they do. Shiny new toys and all that. But then you kind of reach this point where you see that those things come with a whole lot of emptiness if they don't have anything real attached to them. You and Lexie, y'all are putting the "real" into what had started to feel like a fairly shallow existence to me. I think everyday I'm realizing a little more just how shallow it had gotten."

"Compared to what you've done for us, Thomas—"

He stops me there with a raised hand. "It's equal. Okay?"

I don't agree, and I don't guess I ever will, but I stay silent just because I know he doesn't want to hear me say it.

"So how many demos do you have under your belt now?" he asks in a clear change of subject.

"Twenty, but who's counting?"

We smile at each other, and he says, "That's really cool. I hear you're knocking them out of the ballpark."

"I'd be pretty foolish not to give it everything I've got."

"I never doubted that you would. Lila?"

"Yeah?" I reply softly.

"I know I agreed to put the personal stuff on hold for a while, but for the record, it's not what I want."

I don't know how to respond, so I stay quiet for a too-long-stretch of moments, while the night plays out its sounds around us. A dog barks from a house not too far away. Some kind of night bird sings from a nearby tree at the far corner of the yard.

Thomas gets up from his chair and walks over to mine. He squats down next to me. "Are you ever going to let us take a shot at this?"

My fingers literally itch to slide their way through his dark hair. He's wearing this light blue shirt that is one of my favorites on him. And he smells so amazing. A clean, masculine scent that I find rising up in my memory sometimes when I'm in a studio, getting ready to sing a song. I close my eyes, and the scent comes to me, as if it's been imprinted there.

"Thomas," I say, his name a plea to let me escape the position he's putting me in. "I don't want to mess any of this up. How often do relationships last these days? And especially when they come with circumstances like ours?"

"What circumstances?" he asks.

"Challenges. Difficulties."

"You mean Lexie?" he asks.

I shake my head.

"What then?"

I'm silent for a few moments before finally saying, "We can't walk down the street without a woman looking at you in a way that tells me exactly what she would do if I weren't there beside you."

"Is that jealousy I hear?"

"No, it's reality."

"Lila, they're really not looking at me. They're looking at someone they've seen on stage or heard on the radio."

"They look like they want to lick your whole body."

He smiles and shrugs. "Have you asked yourself whether I want them to or not?"

"Well, I know you don't with me standing right there beside you," I rationalize.

"And that's because you're the one that I want there. Not some strange woman I've never met and don't even know."

"I'm just saying we'll be risking a lot if we try to turn this into something that's not really going to have a chance of being."

"So you're not even willing to give us a shot?"

I look into his imploring eyes and, for the life of me, I cannot stop myself from what I am about to do. I lean in and press my lips against his. A soft sound of defeat slips free of me. I slip my arms around his neck and lock them tight.

Thomas clamps his hands onto my waist and lifts me out of the chair. All of a sudden, I am sitting on his lap and I have no idea how he is managing to balance this position. But I don't care because all I want is to get closer to him.

I wrap my legs around his waist, and all of a sudden, we're falling backwards onto the brown pebble terrace. Thomas lands hard, a whooomph of air instantly releasing from his chest. We are both laughing now, a great big burst of it that continues on until my stomach literally hurts with it.

We're flat on our backs, looking up at the star-dotted sky.

"Romance in action," Thomas says. "That's what that was."

I snort a laugh again.

"Oh, you think it's funny, do you?" he says, turning onto his side and draping a leg across mine.

And then he's kissing me this time, but there's nothing testing about it. This kiss means business, and I have not an ounce of will to resist.

As kissing goes, on a scale of one to ten, this would be somewhere around twenty-five. Of course, we've done some passionate kissing before. But the night Thomas and I spent together was a night shared by two people who knew absolutely nothing about each other and had no speck of common history. We simply indulged ourselves in purely physical need.

I guess if I'm honest, part of mine was emotional, but I can't imagine what I was ever thinking to seek that from someone I did not know.

Making love with Thomas had been pleasurable in the most carnal sense of the word, but there had been no substance to it, only awareness of the superficial nature of it. Unlike now when the mingling of physical need and mutual respect and appreciation combine to completely redefine my attraction to him.

He slides fully across me now, and we kiss with bold, outright abandon. Our hands are everywhere, mine sliding under his shirt, his down the back of my jeans. Pressing me as close as it is possible for two people to be when they're still wearing clothes.

And we're both breathing as if we've just climbed a tall mountain and are now at the top, gasping for oxygen.

I hear something coming from inside the house and go completely still, forcing myself to prop up on my elbows and say, "What was that?"

"What?" Thomas says, sounding as if he's been drugged and dragged back to lucidity.

I hear the sound again and then realize it's Lexie on the monitor we had placed in the kitchen so we could hear her from her room if she needed anything.

Thomas realizes it at the same instant, and we both struggle to get up, the rock beneath our feet making us slide and bump into each other. I try to right my clothes as I run into the house, Thomas right behind me.

I hear the crying sound coming through the monitor, and all of a sudden, I cannot get to her room fast enough. I turn the knob and shove the door open.

Lexie is lying on the floor next to her bed, sobbing. "Oh, baby," I say, running over and dropping onto my knees beside her. I slip my arms around her shoulders and lift her to me. "Are you okay? Are you all right?"

She's still sobbing when Thomas drops down beside us and begins running his hands over her arms and back. "Are you hurt, honey? Does anything hurt?"

She buries her face against my chest. I feel her shake her head a little. No.

"Did you have a bad dream, sweetie?"

She nods, and I say, "I'm so sorry. We're right here. There's nothing to be afraid of, okay?"

Thomas stands up and leans over to take her out of my arms, lifting her effortlessly and placing her on the bed. "Everything's all right, baby. Nothing to worry about. Did I ever tell you about the time I fell out of bed when I was a little boy?"

She opens her eyes then and looks at him, her sobs reducing to sniffles.

"Well, if you think this was something, let me tell you. I had this cat named Homer. Big fluffy, yellow cat. Kind of ruled the house if you know what I mean. Like if there was a chair he wanted to sit in, we knew better than to try and scoot him out."

She's fully latched onto every word now. Thomas runs his hand through her silky blonde hair and then continues.

"So he had this pillow. This favorite pillow he liked to sleep on right beside my bed. It was pink, this pillow, which I thought was kind of interesting since he was such a tough kitty. And I wasn't that crazy about having pink in my room, but if I ever tried to sneak the pillow out, he would sit next to my bed and yowl until I put it back again."

Lexie giggles.

"So one night, I was fast asleep when the smoke alarm went off in my house. You know what kind of noise those things make? They could wake you from a coma. From a dead sleep, I bolted up and rolled off my bed. My big toe got hooked in one of the fringy things on Homer's pink pillow. And when I jerked my foot back, the pillow stayed attached to my big toe. The only problem was Homer was also on the pillow. Have you ever seen a cat climb a tree when a dog is chasing it? Well, that's how Homer climbed me. Straight up the front of my pajama pants. Straight up the front of my T-shirt. Until he made himself a perch on top of my head. Guess what it was that kept him there? You got it. I had twenty little cat claw holes in my head by the time the two of us got outside to discover the whole thing had been a false alarm. It sure did give my family a good laugh. The sight of me running outside into the night with Homer on top of my head."

I'm laughing now, belly laughing. And so is Lexie. In fact, we laugh until we're both crying. Thomas just shakes his head, impulsively leaning over to give Lexie a kiss on her no longer tear-stained cheek.

And as my laughter fades and my gaze settles on this man in front of me, there is only one thing I know for sure.

Resisting him is impossible. Why bother to even try?

♪

Thomas

See It Clearly

IT WAS AFTER that night when Lexie fell out of bed that I began to wonder if Lila might be right.

This life we're making together, temporary though we've both labeled it, is a good life. Not a good life, actually. It's a great life.

I don't think either one of us is going to waste any time trying to pretend we aren't crazy-attracted to each other. Every time I walk by Lila, all I want is to grab her and pick up where we left off that night on the terrace. But then I think about those minutes when we had comforted our child together as partners, as a team, as a real mother and father. This fear comes over me, fear of losing that, of losing Lexie, of losing Lila.

Should this be enough? Keep what we have? Let other people fill our physical needs?

But no sooner does that thought run through my mind than I instantly realize I am not in the least attracted to any other woman. It's as if Lila has penetrated my heart and my brain to the point that I have no interest in even looking at anyone else.

That's the part that doesn't exactly seem fair. And the part I'm elaborating on to Holden one afternoon when we're having lunch at a favorite diner near Music Row. CeCe is laying down a vocal at our label's studio. The two of us slipped out to get some food.

Holden leans back in his chair and gives me a long questioning stare. "So what you're telling me is that you're thinking now you and Lila should just be friends. No sex?"

"Yeah," I say evenly, as if I think it's a perfectly plausible solution.

"Have you forgotten about the part where you really like sex?" Holden asks.

"No," I say, letting my irritation show. "I haven't forgotten about that part."

"So are you considering the Benedictine order—"

"Shuutt up," I say, rolling my eyes.

Holden laughs. "Well, if you're committing to no sex, I'm pretty sure you're going to have to become a monk."

"Do I really deserve a jerk for a best friend?"

"Just tryin' to help you see it clearly, man."

"I don't want to mess any of it up, Holden."

"I think the old saying is fish or cut bait. And you don't think there can be anything in between?"

"Yeah, but not if you're both lusting after each other."

"Who says we're lusting?"

"All a person has to do is walk in a room with you two and the pheromones are thick enough to knock you over.

"You read too much."

"Have you ever thought maybe you two should not be living together?"

"Of course I've thought about it. But I like having them there."

"If you and Lila share custody of Lexie, you could take turns."

"Doesn't that sound perfectly awful?" I ask.

"Well, a lot of the world's doing it."

"That doesn't mean it's the way I want to live."

"I get that. But it might come to the point where you don't actually have a choice. Can I ask you something, Thomas?"

"Yeah," I say, shrugging.

"If it weren't for Lexie, would you still have feelings for Lila?"

"It's weird. What I feel for Lila is separate from Lexie, partly about Lexie, partly about the two of them together. It's more than just that one piece of it. That's what makes it seem so incredibly rare and worthy of protection."

"Dude, you have it bad."

"Yeah," I say. "It would appear so."

"Maybe the thing to do," Holden says after a minute, "is to just let it be what it is for now. CeCe's a firm believer in that old adage 'if it's meant to be, it will be.' I guess she's kinda sold me on it."

"It's the waiting part that gets you though."

"Well, yeah, neither one of us has ever been very good at that."

Two teenage girls walk up to our table and say, "Excuse me," in polite Southern voices. Holden and I look up at them, their nervousness palpable.

"Could we please get your autographs?" they say in unison.

"Well, sure thing," Holden says, immediately giving them a smile that makes a fan of his a fan for life.

"Oh, my gosh, we just love your music," the taller girl says. "When will you have a new album out?"

"We're working on that," Holden says, leaning over to sign the back of her T-shirt.

"We can't wait! Y'all's songs are just amazing!"

"We really appreciate that," I say, taking the pen when it's my turn to sign.

They ask us about our next tour, and after another minute or two of small talk, they thank us in their high-pitched teenage voices and bounce off.

"Are we getting older or are our fans getting younger?"

"Huh, you might be getting older," Holden says.

"Are you happy with the way the record's going?" I ask, leaning forward and propping my elbows on the table, glad for a moment to take the focus off my love life, or rather my non-existent love life.

"I think it's the best work we've done yet," Holden says, serious. "Do I think the label's going to get behind it? I really don't know."

"If that's the case, shouldn't we just be putting crap songs on this one, finishing out the contract and saving the good stuff for an independent effort?"

"If we were assholes, yes, I guess that's what we would do."

"Good-faith effort and all that."

"Maybe they'll surprise us," Holden says. "Decide to actually climb on board the new band wagon instead of trying to ride the same old dinosaur."

My gaze widens. "Whoa. I've never heard you talk like that about the label."

"Up until a year or so ago, they were making admirable efforts to keep up with the changes, but I don't see that now. I see digging in heels and insisting on selling music the way it's always been sold. Except that people don't want to buy it that way anymore."

"I guess that's pretty much going to leave us in a pickle sooner or later, huh?"

"Radio is still a predominant way that people hear new music. But independent artists are getting played on radio all the time. A few years ago, that was one of the main things the label could give us that we couldn't get for ourselves. Now, we're pretty much doing most of the legwork for promotion anyway. Interacting with fans on Facebook and Twitter and YouTube. Not only are they not bringing much of that to the table, I think they're actually costing us by holding back on exposure on some of the new streaming services. You gotta admit, once something catches on with people, you can either hop on and get carried along with the tide or stand in the way and get flattened by it."

"Are you saying we're about to get flattened?"

"I wouldn't go that far yet, but it's sure not feeling good to me. I'm hearing new artists all the time who are just tearing it up because they're writing and releasing the stuff that really makes them who they are. It's not filtered by anyone's interpretation of what will sell or not sell."

"Are you saying you're not writing what you want to write?"

"I am. But it's definitely filtered. It has to be when you're playing with somebody else's money and they've told you what the rules are."

"So why don't we just take our toys and go home?" I say.

"Well, we have to get our timing right," Holden allows. "It's not like we don't have anything to lose. And I'm not too anxious to go back to writing songs I can't get anybody to listen to. Much less sing."

"I'd say you're a little bit beyond that, buddy."

"Things can always go south."

"Well, whatever you think. Whatever you decide seems best," I say. "You know I'm with you. I'll keep singing your songs even if nobody's paying me."

"Thanks, man. And I'll keep writing them for you."

♪

Lila

On the Ledge

IT'S THE THIRD SONG I've done for Taylor Pendleton.

I like his writing. His lyrics are words a woman would actually want to sing about herself.

We're taking a break while Joe fine-tunes a couple of things on the track when I tell Taylor this.

"Do you not find it hard to write from a woman's point of view?" I ask him.

He's sitting across the small table from me, sipping on bottled water. He sets it down and says, "I grew up with six sisters."

"Ah. That would explain it."

"I'm not sure there's a situation where I couldn't fill in the blank with what their point of view would be."

"Well, that definitely comes in handy for your profession."

"You use what you got," he says, smiling.

"How long have you been writing?" I ask.

"I was twelve when I started taking guitar lessons. It was just something from the very beginning where I liked picking out melody patterns and then attaching words to them."

"You definitely have a gift," I say.

"Thanks. So do you," he says.

I notice the note in his voice the moment it changes. It's not as if I haven't already picked up on a little something. I've caught him staring at me a few times when I've been in the sound booth, trying to nail a melody. But so far, I've managed to avoid acknowledging my awareness of it. It's impossible to do so now because we're looking straight at each other. I'd have to be dense not to see it written on his face. I glance down at my hands, suddenly at a loss for words.

"What's your story, Lila?" he asks softly.

"Nothing too exciting," I say.

"When did you start singing?"

"Young. Same as you."

"When did you decide to move to Nashville?"

"I wanted to a long time ago, but that wasn't the right time."

"You have an incredible voice," he says.

"Thank you. But most singers in this town do," I say.

"Not everybody," he disagrees. "And most of them don't sound like you."

"That's really nice."

"I'm not saying it to be nice. I'm saying it because it's true." He hesitates, and then, "I realize we haven't known each other very long, and maybe this is a little forward, but I was wondering if you would be interested in doing a video for the first song you demoed for me. 'Sweet Tea and Me.' And possibly getting it out there, on iTunes and such, and see how we do with it."

I sit back a little and stare at him for a few moments, not sure what to say.

"I mean," he says, "I assume you're working on building a singing career of your own."

I shake my head a little. "Right now, I've just been grateful to have the demo work. It's wonderful, and if it doesn't go beyond this, it's still more than I ever dreamed I'd actually get to do."

"Lila, you're way better than doing demo work the rest of your career. I don't have much to offer you at this point. A percentage of royalties and your name on the single as the artist. But it's a new world out there, and YouTube has sold more than a few new artists to the masses."

"I—wow. Thank you, Taylor. I can't say how much I appreciate your thinking of me. But I'm sure you've worked with more experienced singers."

"More experienced, maybe, but I like your sound, Lila. I like it when you sing my songs."

We study each other for a long moment, and I think how smart I would be to fall for someone like him. A guy that I have the love of music in common with. A really good-looking guy, who under any other circumstances, I would have looked more than twice at. "Taylor, I—"

"Look, Lila," he says, interrupting me. "I'm definitely getting the vibe that you're not interested in anything beyond working together. That's cool. I don't know what else you've got going in your life, but I mean what I said about really liking the way you sing my songs. A friend of mine makes videos. He's actually really good. He'd like to do one for this song as kind of a showcase piece for his work. And I'd love it if you would be a part of it."

I feel the excuses I could make rising up inside me. I'm about to voice them when I realize that this is an opportunity and I'm pretty sure it's one I should take. I shake my head a little and say, "Thank you, Taylor. Really. If you think this is something I can do in a way you would be pleased with where your song is concerned, then, yes, I'd love to."

♪

SO I TELL THOMAS about it at dinner that night.

I realize as soon as I start in that I'm having trouble saying what it is I'm trying to say without stumbling over my words.

I finally do get them out, but then I can see Thomas's deliberate attempt to respond in a positive way.

"That's great, Lila. Do you like the song?"

"Yeah. Actually, I really like the song."

"Who's the writer?"

"Taylor Pendleton."

"I haven't heard of him," Thomas says, his response containing a slight edge.

I'm quiet for a moment, and then say, "He's probably only a little less green than I am. Anyway, his friend is a videographer, and they're planning to shoot the video next Friday."

"Where will the shooting be?" Thomas asks.

"Somewhere outside the city. I forget the name of the lake."

"Lake Tilmer?"

I nod yes, that's it. "I'm not sure how long it will run that day. Do you think you'll be able to get Lexie—"

"Yeah," he says. "Sure."

He's quiet as we carry our dishes into the kitchen and put them in the dishwasher. "Is anything wrong?" I finally ask.

"No, nothing's wrong," he says.

"Do you think this is a bad idea?"

He shakes his head. "If you like his work, and he seems like a keep-his-word kind of guy, it'll probably be a good experience."

"Okay. Good."

"If you don't need any help with anything, I'm going out for a bit. Be back a little later."

"Okay," I say, surprised, but trying not to show it.

He walks out of the kitchen then, his booted steps making a hollow sound on the marble floor. I hear him grab his keys from the bowl near the front door and wait for the start of the truck. I listen as he backs out of the driveway.

I finish tidying up the kitchen, check on Lexie who's already asleep and then run myself a hot bath. I pour in some bath salts and slide into the tub, leaning my head back and trying to think what it is about my doing this video that would bother Thomas so much.

Could it be jealousy of Taylor? I think about it for a moment and decide that it seems like the only plausible explanation.

If Thomas only knew.

If he had any idea how many times a day I think about him, how I go to sleep every night with this ache in the center of my chest that starts every time I remember the night out on the terrace. The way he kissed me. The way he held me.

Sometimes, it feels like I'm addicted to some drug that my body absolutely craves to the point of insanity. And I cannot think of anything else.

But I continue to talk myself off that particular ledge by remembering everything I have to lose. I know better than to kid myself about what it is that Thomas sees in me. I'm not going to deny that there's physical attraction on both our parts.

But I suspect he's been physically attracted to a lot of girls in his life. I really don't see me being the last one.

I'm not saying this because I feel sorry for myself where this reality is concerned. I think it's just something that will almost for sure turn out to be true.

And so, giving in to my own desire to be with Thomas again seems more than a little short-sighted.

Wouldn't it be best if we both found someone else now? Someone to dilute this build-up of want between us? Not that I want anyone else. But what if I let Thomas think I do?

Wouldn't that give him the incentive to move on? And wouldn't that be the best thing?'

But as I sit here in the tub, I really can't imagine doing that. It sounds so conniving and manipulative.

And really, that's so far from my intent.

I find myself wondering then, what would it hurt, or who would it hurt, if I slipped into Thomas's bed and waited for him to get back tonight? Other than the two of us, who would know? And what if it doesn't ruin everything? What if it makes it better? What if I'm insisting on something that is shortchanging us both?

I close my eyes and actually envision doing what I've just thought about doing. Sliding out of my clothes and into Thomas's bed with its slick satin sheets. I imagine the look on his face when he finds me there.

And I realize that's exactly what I want to do. Crazy as it sounds, it's what I want to do.

So I shave my legs until they're smooth as butter. I rub coconut oil over my entire body and then rinse it off until it leaves behind nothing but softness.

I step out of the bathtub, reaching for a towel. I stand in front of the mirror, dropping it and wondering if I still look the way he remembers me.

Without vanity, I think I can say I look pretty much the same. Not the prettiest girl he's ever been with. But maybe whatever he saw in me is still there.

I slip into my robe, go to Lexie's room and double-check to make sure she's still asleep.

I walk down the hall to the far end and open the door to Thomas's room.

A lamp is on by the bed. I walk over, flick it off, and pull back the covers. I untie my robe and let it fall from my shoulders onto the floor.

And I wait.

♪

Thomas

A Ride Home

I DECIDE TO pull a good drunk by myself in the back of the little bar near Vanderbilt. As it turns out, alcohol does little to dilute what I reluctantly admit is jealousy about Lila working with a writer she obviously admires.

I know I'm being a jerk, and after the fourth beer, I decide to pay my tab and head home.

Just as I step up to the bar, two college-age girls walk over and introduce themselves.

"I'm Ally," the bolder of the two says. "And this is my friend, Ginny."

"How y'all doing? I was just heading out."

"Yeah," Ally says. "About that. We'd be happy to drive you home. We noticed you had a bit to drink. And there are lots of traffic checks around here." She looks at me with blue eyes that are actually not flirtatious but concerned.

"Yeah," Ginny says. "You wouldn't want to show up in the paper tomorrow with a DUI."

I start to deny my intoxication, but realize I wouldn't be fooling them. "I can get a cab home," I say.

"Aw, we'd like to drive you," Ally says. "Do you know how many songs we've absolutely loved of yours?"

"And we promise not to take advantage of you," Ginny chimes in.

They both giggle then, and I smile back at them, shaking my head. "I can call a friend."

"Noo, please," Ally pleads. "Let us do it. We'll have something to tell our friends for weeks."

As ridiculous as it sounds to me, I can see they really do mean it. I fish my keys out of my pocket and hand them over.

Less than fifteen minutes later, we're making the turn into the driveway of my house. Ally is driving. She takes the turn into the driveway a little too fast. The front end nosedives and makes a loud, scraping noise.

"Oh, my goodness," she says. "I'm so sorry."

"Don't worry about it," I say. "It's not the first time."

But her cheeks are flame red when she puts the truck in park and turns off the ignition. "I hope it didn't mess anything up," she says.

"I'm sure it's fine," I say, opening the door and stepping out.

The girls slide out of the truck as well. "The taxi you called for us should be here anytime, but would you mind if we get a selfie with you?"

"Not at all," I say, rubbing a hand across my jaw. "If you don't mind all this stubble."

"Not one bit," Ginny says.

They're both giggling as I get in between them, putting an arm around their shoulders. We do a few goofy poses and then one where I try to look like the country music star they want to show their friends.

"Thank you, Thomas," they both say, and then each of them stands on tiptoe to kiss me on the cheek.

The taxi rolls up, and I walk them down to the end of the driveway, thank them for their kindness and pay the driver. "You'll get them safely back to Vanderbilt?" I ask him.

"Sure thing," he says, and as he drives off, they wave through the back window.

I head for the kitchen and pour myself an enormous glass of water, drinking every last drop in an effort to avoid the headache I do not want tomorrow.

I take Brownie out for a quick pee, and then ten minutes later, stick my head inside Lexie's room and see her curled up on her pillow. I close the door quietly behind me and force myself to walk straight past Lila's door to my own room.

I walk to the bed and turn on the lamp on the nightstand, immediately noticing that the bed isn't made. The housekeeper had been in that morning and she always leaves the bed military-style neat.

That's strange. I know Lexie couldn't have come in here by herself and that only leaves Lila.

I sit down on the mattress, lean in and catch a whiff of her scent from the pillow. I breathe in the familiar smell. I pull the blanket back and see that the sheet is damp.

Had Lila been in here, and if so, why? Had she been waiting for me? And then I realize that she must have heard the girls giggling outside and left the room.

I throw myself back on the mattress, arms splayed above my head. Damn, Franklin. You really blew it this time.

♪

Lila

Mortification

I AM CURLED up in a tight ball under the covers of my bed.

When I hear Thomas's footsteps in the hallway, pausing for a second outside my door, I pray that he will not knock. I could not face him right now for all the money in the world. Mortified does not begin to describe my current state.

What on earth had I been thinking? My face still feels like it's on fire. I am such an idiot.

I had decided to ignore my own recognition of the fact that this is part of Thomas's life. Girls, women throwing themselves at him.

And here I am, thinking he left the house because he was jealous of me spending time with someone else. When in truth, I guess he had not cared at all.

As soon as I'm sure he's in his room, I get out of bed and search through a drawer for my most matronly pajamas. I slip them on and button the top all the way to the neck and then get back in bed, feeling myself start to sweat. But, that's okay. I deserve it for trying to act like a sexpot, when I am clearly not.

At least, thank goodness, I got out of the room before he ever realized I was there. I can only hope he was too drunk to notice the bed was unmade.

♪

Thomas

Where She Has Been

IT'S ALL BUT torturous lying here between these sheets, where I know she has been. Wondering what she was wearing. If she was wearing anything at all.

For the life of me, I cannot go to sleep. I finally launch myself out of bed and turn on the shower, setting the water to the coldest setting I think I can stand. I step under the spray and stand there until my teeth start to chatter, and I have nearly turned myself into an ice cube.

Only then, do I get out, dry off and head back to bed.

♪

Lila

Avoidance

I KNOCK AT Thomas's door at just after seven when he hasn't made an appearance in the kitchen, and it's almost time to leave to take Lexie to school.

I open the door a little more than a crack and, without sticking my head in, say, "Do you mind if I use the truck to take Lexie?"

"Oh, heck," he says, and I hear him leap out of bed. "Did I oversleep?"

"It's okay," I say, glad that we won't have to face each other at least. "Really."

"I can be ready in five minutes," he says.

"It's fine. I've got it if you don't mind me driving the truck."

"Of course not."

"Thank you," I say, my voice strained even as I'm trying to sound neutral.

I gather up Lexie's things and help her into her chair. We've just gotten outside when I hear the front door of the house open. I glance over my shoulder to find Thomas jogging up, a look of apology on his face.

"I forgot about the chair," he says, lifting it up into the back of the truck.

He helps get everything inside, including Lexie, buckling her seat belt and then turning to look at me.

"I'll come too," he says.

"No," I say, more sharply than I'd intended. "They have the helper at the front door. I'll just ask him."

A look of hurt crosses Thomas's face, and I suddenly wish I could take the words back. But then I remember my humiliation from the night before, and I can't bring myself to look at him another moment.

I walk around and get in the driver's side. Thomas waves at Lexie and she raises her small hand at him. She looks at me then as if she knows something isn't quite right. I force myself to make small talk all the way to school, telling her what I have planned for my day.

It's not until I've delivered her safely to the front door of the school and watched her be wheeled inside that I let the tears roll up and out of me.

I have no reason whatsoever to be crying. I haven't lost anything that I ever actually had. Well, except for those few moments last night when I had decided to go against my better judgment. When I had very nearly made a fool of myself.

At least I had been spared that.

I stop at Starbucks, go in the restroom and wash my face. I stay there until I'm sure I'm not going to cry again. I order coffee and sit down to drink it.

By the time I get back home, Thomas has gone out for a run, according to the note on the kitchen counter. CeCe had offered to pick me up this morning and drive me to another studio on Music Row for an introduction to a producer. I get dressed quickly, putting on some makeup and lipstick. I wait outside the house until CeCe arrives.

She's backing out of the driveway just as Thomas rounds the corner on the sidewalk near the house. She blows her horn and waves. He lifts a hand and waves back.

"Do you want to stop?" she asks me.

"Better not," I say. "We might be late."

♪

WE MANAGE TO AVOID each other for the next few days. I'm not sure who's making more effort where that's concerned, me or Thomas.

And so, by the time Friday arrives, the day of the video shoot, we haven't talked about it again. In fact, on Friday morning, I help Lexie get ready and make her breakfast. The plan was for Thomas to drive her today and to pick her up.

"Got a kiss for Mama?" he asks, picking her up from the chair at the kitchen table.

She lifts her arms to me, and I lean over and hug her, hard. "I hope you have a wonderful day," I say. "I'll see you tonight, okay?"

Thomas carries her out of the kitchen then, out to the truck, and I watch from the front door, realizing that this day felt so much more exciting when I had Thomas to share it with.

♪

TAYLOR PICKS ME up about ten minutes after Thomas leaves the house with Lexie. He had not asked how I would be getting to the shoot, and I didn't volunteer the information. But I'm glad that he's not back when we pull out of the driveway.

Taylor's Wrangler Jeep is open on the sides, and I welcome the air blowing against the heat in my cheeks.

"Everything all right?" Taylor asks, glancing at me with a look of uncertainty.

"Yeah, I'm fine," I say, running a hand through my hair. "Little bit of a hectic morning."

We drive for thirty seconds or so without saying anything, but the silence is heavy. I can feel his curiosity, so I'm not surprised when he says, "Pretty awesome neighborhood. Pretty awesome house."

"It's not mine," I say.

"Yeah, I've driven by here before. That's Thomas Franklin's house, right?"

"Yes, it is." I could leave it at that, offer up no more information. But if Taylor and I are going to be working together, the truth will come out eventually anyway, so I say, "It's kind of complicated. Thomas and I knew each other a long time ago. We have a daughter together. She and I are just staying with him until we can get on our own feet here."

He leans back in the seat a bit, his eyes going wide. I don't suppose I could have said anything that would have surprised him more.

"Whoa. And here I was thinking you were all unconnected and everything. You probably didn't really need to do this shoot, did you?" he says, sounding a little embarrassed now.

"No, I mean yes, I do need to do it. I want to do it. Thomas has a great career, something he's worked really hard for. But that doesn't have anything to do with me. Whatever I accomplish or don't accomplish here, I want to do on my own. Although, in all honesty, CeCe MacKenzie put in a good word for me with Joe, and that's how I started getting demo work."

"You would have been able to do that on your own. I'm sure you've heard it before, but this is a town built on relationships. When someone likes you and wants to do something nice for you, you learn to let them. And then when you have the opportunity to do something nice for someone else, you do. It makes it an awfully nice place to live."

We're quiet for a mile or so before he adds, "So you and Thomas . . . are you—"

"No," I say. "We're trying to figure out how to raise our daughter together, but as for anything else, we're both single."

Taylor brightens at this.

I should probably choose this opportunity to reinforce my 'let's keep this platonic position,' but he's such a good guy, and I don't know, I guess my ego is feeling more than a little dented right now.

He begins telling me about the video shoot then, and I hear the excitement in his voice. I start to get excited too.

By the time we arrive there, forty minutes outside the city, I feel like I've already been given a tour of the place, because it is exactly as Taylor had described it.

The house is a two-story white farmhouse surrounded by an enormous flat green yard. Flowers of every imaginable color have been planted in so many different places that my eyes don't know where to settle first.

The house belongs to another friend of Taylor's, and it really is the perfect fit for the song. The front door is open. We walk inside, through the living room and a set of pane-glass doors, then off a porch that leads to more grass and the lake beyond.

Taylor puts a hand to my elbow as we approach the group of people standing close to the water's edge. A guy somewhere around our age steps forward, slaps Taylor on the shoulder and reaches out a hand to me.

"You must be Lila," he says.

"Lila, this is Marshall Henry," Taylor says. "Marshall, Lila Bellamy."

"Hi, Marshall," I say. "It's really nice to meet you."

"Great to meet you," he says, smiling a genuine smile of welcome. "We've got the perfect day for it. Y'all ready to get started?"

"Yeah," Taylor says. "Just put us where you need us."

♪

IT SEEMS LIKE I blink and ten hours have passed since we got to the house. The day is full, but it's been a long time since I've enjoyed anything so much.

The crew for the shoot are all friends of either Taylor or Marshall, and everyone is volunteering their time in exchange for some barter system they've set up with each other, which I think is really cool. Trading talent for talent.

There are some scenes when I'm singing on the dock, one on a boat out on the lake, and a few in the grass by the shoreline. It feels far more like play than work, and I feel guilty at the thought of receiving any kind of pay for doing this. Here in this beautiful place, singing a song I really like, changing into different outfits—it's more like a game of dress-up than work.

But both Taylor and Marshall seem pleased with the results we're getting. And I do give every shot my best, wanting to make sure they don't regret asking me to do this.

It's after eight by the time Marshall calls everything a wrap. It's a little sad saying good-bye to everyone, something about the way we'd all worked together today creating a mini-world of our own during these hours.

I exchanged texts with Thomas earlier, making sure he had picked up Lexie. He didn't ask when I would be home. I didn't volunteer the information since I didn't know exactly what time it would be anyway. Thomas's answers were short and to the point, and it stung a little that he didn't ask about the shoot. But then compared to what he's used to, today would fall under the heading of small potatoes.

I think I'm being a little self-centered to think it would be interesting to him.

We've just left the farmhouse, heading back to Nashville when Taylor looks at me and says, "So what did you think? Really?"

"I loved it," I say.

"I did too," he admits, sounding a little like a kid who got the toy he most wanted for Christmas. "You were incredible, Lila. You kind of shine on camera, do you know that?"

"No," I say, "but it's probably Marshall's touch-up work or something."

"Nothing was touched up. It's pretty cool to see something you've created come to life the way I got to do today. You kind of imagine what a song will end up sounding like with your ideal person singing it. And then what it would look like as a video with real people. I have to tell you, I couldn't have imagined it any better."

I look down at my hands and say, "You're being incredibly kind. I'm just so happy I got to be a part of it."

We don't talk much for the rest of the way into the city. It's as if we're both absorbing the fullness of the day and the satisfaction of knowing it had been as much as either of us had hoped for.

We're a couple of miles from Thomas's house when Taylor looks at me and says, "Can I be bold for a moment?"

"Yeah," I say.

"I'm not a pushy guy, and when I've been given a hint, I'm really good at taking it. At the same time, I know a good thing when I see it. Or feel it, anyway. If there comes a point where you decide that this single thing isn't working for you anymore, and you'd be open to someone in your life, I'd really welcome the opportunity to be considered."

I smile at his phrasing, shaking my head a little. "Taylor, I think we're at pretty different points in our lives."

"We're virtually the same age," he says, shrugging his shoulders.

"Age doesn't really have anything to do with it," I say. "I have a daughter."

"I know," he says, interrupting me, "which I think is really cool. I love kids."

I'm silent for a moment and then say, "Lexie is special. She has cerebral palsy and needs a lot more from me than a child her age normally would."

"Hey," Taylor says, reaching across to place his hand over mine. "I'm sorry. I didn't know."

"Don't be. It's not like that. It's all good. She's wonderful. She's the joy of my life, and I can't imagine living a single day without her. But I guess what I was trying to say is sometimes I feel a lot older than my age. I don't know, like maybe I don't know how to be lighthearted anymore."

"Because you've been responsible for so long," he says.

"Yeah. I guess so."

"Which makes you awesome," he says. "I admire you, Lila, for doing what you've done and still being willing to go after your own dream. A lot of people would have skipped one or the other. It's hard to do the right thing. My mom had me when she was seventeen. She had dreams of being an actress. Turns out, she really didn't want a kid so she moved to LA and my grandmother raised me."

His hand is on mine. I slip my fingers through his, needing connection in this moment as much as I suspect he needs it as well. "I'm glad you had your grandmother," I say.

"Me too. She was probably one of the best people to ever live on this earth. I couldn't be any more grateful for what she's done for me. But you know there's always that thing in the back of your mind where you wonder why you weren't enough for your mother. Why she didn't want to be with you."

I tighten my grip on his hand and don't try to diminish what he's just said. "It hurts," I say.

"Yeah," he says, making an attempt to lighten his voice. "It does."

"Do you ever see your mother?" I ask.

"Ah, she died when I was twelve. Of an overdose."

"I'm so sorry, Taylor."

"Thanks," he says. "I wish things could have turned out a little differently. That we'd had the opportunity for some closure."

There's pain in his voice now. When I ask him to pull the car over, I'm not sure exactly why I'm doing it. But he does, turning into the parking lot of a store that's already closed for the night. He puts the Jeep in park and turns to face me. We look at each other for what feels like a really long time. I reach out and cup my hand to the side of his face.

"Lila," he says. My name is a mixture of longing and disbelief and desire. And I guess that's what I need to hear. I lean across and kiss him. Because I want to. Not because I feel sorry for him or think I can temporarily make him feel better. Painful places know painful places. I've felt so much of what I heard in his voice just a few minutes ago.

It's not long before he takes over the lead and presses me back against the door on my side of the car, following me until he's halfway in my seat. And we are kissing with the kind of hunger that comes from having been empty inside for too long. But when his hands slide beneath my shirt and up my back, I realize this shouldn't go any further. At least not now. I struggle to sit up and say, "Taylor, we should stop."

He goes completely still and draws in a deep breath as if he has to reach deep for the self-control. He slides into his seat and leans his head back, looking up at the sky through the open sun-roof. "One and a thousand, two and a thousand," he says.

I laugh. "I'm sorry," I say.

"I'm not sorry," he says. "This might just be the best day of my life."

And then I start to feel scared, scared that I've let him think something that's probably not going to happen. But I don't know how to take it back. "I just have to get home," I say. "Check on Lexie."

"It's cool," he says, turning on the Jeep and reversing out of the parking lot.

He's smiling though, and the smile doesn't fade the remaining mile to the house. It's still there when he pulls into the driveway, tells me goodnight and thanks me again for the work on the video.

"It was my pleasure," I say. "Thank you for the day."

I find it hard to meet his gaze now. I'm not sure what I want to let him see, my enjoyment of the day and his kiss or my worry that I've let something happen we'll both regret. "Goodnight, Taylor."

"'Night, Lila."

I walk to the front door, fish my key out of the side pocket of my purse and turn to wave as he backs out and drives off.

Lamps are on in the house, but the lighting is low. I gasp when Thomas rounds the corner from the kitchen into the hallway. We nearly collide, and I say, "Oh, I'm sorry. I didn't see you there."

We both step back as if we've just touched a hot stove.

"Hey," he says. "How was the shoot?"

"It was great," I say, looking up at him then under the sudden realization that just the scent of him stirs in me an undeniable longing which couldn't be much more wrong since I just made out with another guy.

And then come the comparisons I'd rather not make. Everything about Thomas is larger than life. His voice. His wide shoulders. His broad chest. His long legs. His sexy mouth.

By any definition, Taylor is a good-looking guy, and I do find him attractive. Not just physically. He's the kind of guy you can be around and not be constantly thinking about the bump on your forehead and whether he's going to notice it.

With Thomas, I am aware of every one of my imperfections and how the two of us will never match up in that way. In my eyes, he has no imperfections.

He's looking at me with questions on his face, and I feel them as clearly as if he has voiced them out loud.

"Is Lexie okay?" I ask, trying not to shift my gaze.

"Yeah, she fell asleep around eight-thirty. I think she was tired."

"Me too. I'm going on to bed." I step back and start to turn away from him, but he reaches out and stops me with a hand on my arm.

"Lila, can we talk?"

I force myself to look at him and say, "About what?"

"The way things have been these past few days. I hate it."

I glance down and admit, "I haven't liked it either."

"About the other night, those girls drove me home because I had a little too much to drink. They were just being nice. It was nothing more than that. I promise."

"You don't have to promise me anything," I say.

"I know I don't have to. But I'm telling you the truth."

"Thomas, I think we're proving to ourselves right now why we were right about this not being a good idea. It's been miserable the last few days because of the conflict between us. I know Lexie has felt it. Don't you think it's better for all of us if we just—"

I don't finish the sentence. Thomas hauls me into his arms, locking me against him and kissing me full and deep. But as quickly as he starts this, he ends it, stepping back and holding up both hands. He looks at me with surprise and disappointment and something else I can't name.

"That's not your perfume I smell, is it? It's cologne. His cologne, right?"

My cheeks blaze red hot. "Thomas—"

"Don't, Lila," he says. "Let's just end this here."

He steps back away from me, as if he's sorry he ever touched me. I feel something very much like shame, as if I've been unfaithful to him, which is ridiculous considering that we have no commitment to each other.

I try to think of something to say that doesn't sound like I'm groveling or apologizing for kissing someone else. But then I look at him and what I see on his face isn't anger. It's just hurt. Plain hurt. I realize that's not something I ever wanted to make him feel. It's what I had felt the other night when those girls brought him home, when I had decided to put myself in his bed.

I'd been embarrassed for sure, but above that, more than that, hurt. And even as Thomas turns and walks away from me, long, floor-covering strides away from me, I wonder why we're doing this to each other. I think it is only then that I realize the extent to which he could break my heart if I put myself in the position to let him.

♪

Thomas

A Good Friend to Say It

I DON'T GO looking for it, but I don't turn away from it either. Call it ego. Pride. I don't know. Maybe it's just a desperate need to replace the feel of Lila with someone else in my arms.

I'm in the studio with CeCe and Holden one afternoon a week after my disastrous attempt to kiss Lila. A backup singer who's recording in one of the other studios has come in to chat with CeCe. I notice how she keeps swinging her gaze my way and letting it land on my face, and then on other parts of me as well.

The invitation is undeniable, and I find myself walking over to where the two of them are nursing bottles of water.

"Thomas, do you know Holly?" CeCe asks.

"I don't believe I do," I say.

"Thomas Franklin, Holly Meyers," she says, making the introduction.

"Well, I know who you are," Holly says. "But then who doesn't?" She laughs and sticks her hand into mine.

We shake, and I say, "Nice to meet you, Holly."

I ask her about the record she's working on, polite small talk designed to take the heat out of her gaze. It's pretty ineffective as far as that goes. I kind of force myself to follow her lead, practicing flirting as if I've gotten rusty and forgotten how to do it. But I haven't really forgotten. It's just that my heart isn't in it, and my words sound as flat to me as they no doubt do to her.

CeCe steps away when Holden waves at her from across the room. As soon as she's out of earshot, Holly looks up at me. "Mind if I'm blatantly shameful for a moment?"

"No. Go right ahead."

"I've been trying to get CeCe to introduce you to me for way longer than I care to admit. She's pretty protective of you, you know."

I raise an eyebrow, fold my arms across my chest. "Do I need to be protected from you?"

"Only in the nicest kind of way," she says, laughing.

I smile at this. "I doubt there are too many guys who want to be protected from you, Holly."

"You just don't happen to be one of them, right?"

"It's a little more complicated than that," I say.

"Another woman in the picture? You don't even have to say it. It's written all over your face."

"Hey, now."

"Oh, it's true," she says. "You've got it bad, don't you?"

I start to deny it, but it seems like she has my number and what would be the point anyway?

She draws in a deep breath and releases it in a sigh. "Well, I have to get back to work. If you ever decide she's not the one for you, I'd love a shot at it." She smiles a wide, pretty smile at me and then walks out of the studio.

I wonder if I'm a fool not to go after her.

♪

LATER THAT AFTEROON, we've just finished up the recording session when CeCe leans back in her chair, stretches her long legs out in front of her and says, "So, Holly?"

I lift my shoulders, shrug. "She's nice."

"She is. Which is exactly why I've never introduced her to you."

I look up at her, raise an eyebrow.

"That one was for both her and you."

"How you figure?"

"Because she's not your type."

"Oh, and you're the expert on my type?"

"When you've seen as many flunk the test as I have, you start to form a profile."

"Well, maybe you should let me in on it," I say.

"She's living in your house right now," CeCe says. "She's the only girl I've ever seen who put that look in your eyes."

"What look?"

"Lovesick. Hangdog."

"Okay, now you're being cruel."

She laughs. "Not cruel. Just honest."

"Don't even bother to open up that can of no-good today."

"Which part? The part where you're gonna end up letting somebody else scoop her up?"

"That is not how it is."

"She told me about the video shoot and about Taylor, the writer."

I actually feel the heat blaze in my eyes. "Why the heck do you like to get me so riled up?"

"Somebody needs to."

I stand up. "I gotta go."

"Thomas," she says, putting a hand on my arm to stop me. "Seriously. Sometimes, we need to hear what we don't want to hear. And sometimes, we just need a really good friend to say it. So I'm going to say it. You and Lila, whatever it is you feel for each other, it's based on something real, Thomas. I was lucky enough to find that with Holden. Even in a place, a profession where sometimes, things aren't real at all. If you decide you're going to throw that all away, I just hope you know for sure what it is you're giving up."

♪

Lila

Messy

ON FRIDAY MORNING when I drive Lexie to school in Thomas's truck, I'm so excited I can hardly contain myself.

Macy is coming to town tonight. Thomas, CeCe and Holden left on Wednesday for a week of shows in New York City. And I guess I sounded so glum when Macy called me earlier in the week that she took pity on me and agreed to come for a weekend visit.

I tell Lexie how excited Macy will be to see her. The smile on my daughter's face tells me she's as happy about seeing our friend as I am.

I have two demos to sing at noon. On impulse, afterward, I go to a little shop I found downtown that has really cute clothes that tend to be in my price range.

I end up buying a dress in a pretty shade of blue that hits just above my knees. I decide to pair it with cowboy boots.

Macy arrives at the house just after five. Lexie and I greet her at the door with hugs and kisses. She takes in the house with a look of awe on her face.

"Wow, you two are living the life," she says. "What an incredible place."

Under any other circumstances, I would feel awkward, but Macy knows that I know it isn't mine. And I don't need to explain any of that to her.

"I fixed some dinner for us. A spinach salad with apples and walnuts. Still one of your favorites?"

"You better believe it," Macy says.

We eat at the table on the terrace. Brownie sniffs around the yard, smelling trees and bushes and walking the perimeter of the fenced area with a pride that says he considers it his responsibility to make sure all is well.

Macy watches him for a moment and then looks at me, shaking her head. "It's hard to believe that's the same dog."

"I know," I say.

"There's something different about him. It's like he knows he's loved and valued."

"He is."

"Did I ever tell you that you're amazing?"

"I don't recall it," I say. I smile then and shake my head. "He's done way more for me than I'll ever do for him."

"I doubt that he would agree with you on that."

We sit for a couple of hours, just talking and taking our time eating, Macy telling Lexie silly stories and making her laugh.

At eight o'clock, the babysitter arrives. CeCe had gotten a recommendation from a friend, and I introduce her to Lexie.

"Lexie, this is Madeline."

Madeline high-fives her and pulls out her iPhone to show her a picture of her dog. Lexie points at Brownie and pats the center of her chest. *Mine.*

As if he knows he's being talked about, Brownie waggles over, his tail making a steady swipe, swipe, swipe of approval.

By the time Macy and I finish getting dressed and are ready to leave, I feel completely comfortable about Madeline's connection with Lexie. They're engrossed in some game on her phone. And I'm not sure Lexie even notices when I kiss her on the head and say good-bye.

We're in Macy's car, driving toward downtown when she looks at me and says with a whine in her voice, "I really can't believe how much she has changed in this amount of time. She's growing up."

"I'm afraid there's no slowing that one down," I say.

"She seems so happy."

"She is. School is wonderful for her. They do such amazing things every day."

We drive in silence for a moment before Macy looks at me and then says, "You on the other hand? You don't look so happy."

I glance at her with a purposefully blanked expression. "Things are great, Macy. I am happy."

"So what is it that you and Thomas have worked out?"

"Nothing," I say. "We both take care of Lexie. And other than that, we don't see too much of each other."

"Because?"

"Because we both agree that anything else would just be too messy."

"News flash here. Love is messy. Life is messy."

"And shouldn't you avoid that whenever you can?"

"Yeah, except that messy comes with some pretty amazing bonus points."

"We kind of had an argument," I say.

"About?"

"Let's just say he hurt my feelings, and I hurt his."

"What are y'all? Six?"

I laugh a little at her tone. "I don't think we're meant to be anything other than hit or miss."

"Oh, I don't think he missed," Macy says, laughing.

I smack her arm and roll my eyes. "It's impossible to have an adult conversation with you."

"I'm an adult," Macy protests. "So tell me about tonight. Where are we going?"

"A show at the Bluebird. A writer I've been doing some demo work for is playing with some of his friends there tonight."

"Ohhh. Name, please."

"Taylor. Pendleton." I tell her then about the video, the songs I've been singing for demos and how much I've learned just by being in the studio and getting the opportunity to sing so many different things. "People are amazingly generous, just with time and advice. Things they don't necessarily have to be generous with."

I tell her too about some of the people I've met, and she tells me she's no longer working at Smart-Send and has gotten a job as a receptionist at a local law office.

"Seriously?" I say. "All right, Macy."

"Yeah, it's Mama working her wiles again. She goes to church with this lawyer, and I guess she sang him my sob story. He miraculously found a job opening for me."

"That's wonderful," I say. "I'm so glad you're not at that place anymore."

"I know Bertha and Marsha miss us," she says.

"Yeah, as resident punching bags," I agree and laugh.

At the Bluebird, we wait in line for a few minutes before the doors open, and people start to flow in.

Inside, I spot Taylor and some of his buddies up front. I lead Macy over and introduce her to him, and he introduces us to the other guys he's with.

Macy shakes their hands and gives each of them her perfect Southern-girl smile. When it lands on Taylor, I notice the wattage change a bit.

"Heard a lot about you, Taylor," she says. "Lila sure does like your songs."

"And I like her singing," he says. "What brings you to Nashville, Macy?"

"Spending time with my bestie," she says, pointing at me.

"Y'all going to be around after the show?" Taylor asks, looking at me.

"Yeah, I think so. We're planning to stay for the whole thing."

"How about letting us buy you a beer then?"

"That would be wonderful," Macy says before I can answer.

He smiles, and I notice that his gaze stays on Macy when he says, "Great. That would be great."

♩

THE MUSIC IS amazing, and we both sit at a table up front which Taylor has somehow managed to snag for us.

Macy and I are standing at the bar when Taylor and his friends walk over after they're done playing. Taylor orders each of us a beer, and then one for himself. We stand in a circle and talk about music and YouTube and bad jokes, and it's almost midnight before I realize it.

I tap Macy on the shoulder and tell her I'm going to the restroom to call and check on Lexie.

"Want me to come?" she asks.

"No, I'm good. Back in a minute," I say.

Once I'm away from the noise, I call and speak to Madeline. She assures me she's fine with staying as long as I need her. But I tell her we should be home within an hour or so.

I use the restroom, wash my hands and head back to the bar. Just outside the restroom door, I turn the corner and spot Macy and Taylor laughing at something. Her hand is on his arm, and just the way he's looking at her tells me that he very much likes it.

I wait to see if I feel any kind of disappointment over this realization, but it's not that at all. Taylor is one of the nicest guys I've ever met. Macy is my best friend. If something happens between them, that would be a wonderful thing as far as I'm concerned.

So I fake a headache and tell Macy I'm going to call a cab and head back to the house. She protests at first, saying she'll come with me, but I insist that she stay. And when I glance at Taylor and then give Macy a little smile, I can see that she understands.

♪

THE TAXI ARRIVES in five minutes. As soon as I get inside, I send Macy a text.

He's one of the good ones. Do NOT break his heart.
Me?
Yes, you. Renowned heartbreaker.
I'm afraid this time, I'm the one in danger.

♪

Lila

He's Back

MADELINE IS IN the living room, watching TV when I let myself in the house.

She tells me she really enjoyed spending time with Lexie and hopes I'll call her again. I tell her I will and pay her. She says goodnight and leaves.

I go in and check on Lexie right away, finding her fast asleep, one of the toys Thomas had given her tucked up under her arm. I give her a kiss and smooth her hair back from her face. I let myself out of the room, closing the door quietly behind me.

I change into my pajamas and then go back to the kitchen for something to drink. The doorbell rings. My heart thuds for a moment until I realize it must be Macy.

I start to glance out the window to make sure it's her, but then who else would it be? I pull open the heavy wood door, a smile on my face, and then I scream, and just as quickly, try to slam it.

But the door is heavy, and Rowdy is inside before I can close it even an inch.

He shoves me backward, and I fall hard onto the marble floor, a knife-like pain stabbing through my lower back.

"Hey there, girlie. I guess you're surprised to see me, huh?"

"What are you doing here, Rowdy?" I yell, scrambling away and trying to get to my feet.

He kicks at my ankle with his heavy booted foot and trips me so that I fall to the floor again, this time on my knees.

"That's good practice because by the time I'm through with you, that's exactly where you're going to be. On your knees. Begging."

I scream and start crawling down the hall toward Lexie's room. But I stop because the last thing in the world I want to do is lead him to her.

I try to stand, and this time, he lets me. I run into the kitchen, but he's right behind me.

He reaches out and grabs my hair, yanking me to a full stop. I scream again, this time out of pain.

"Rowdy, please! Don't do this. You need to go."

"I need to go? I just got here, missy. And I ain't leaving until I get what I came for."

He reels me in, still holding onto my hair.

"Why are you here? How did you find me?"

"You should tell your friend not to go blabbing all over town how she's coming to see you. She led me right to your front door."

"You're sick!" I scream.

"Well, I don't know about that. But I do know I'm mad as hell. You and that perfect ass boyfriend of yours, sticking your nose where it don't belong. In a man's private business."

"If you get out of here now, Rowdy, you might not end up back in prison!"

I think about Brownie then, that he's outside in the fenced yard where I let him out to go potty when I got home. I pray that he stays quiet. Please, let him stay quiet.

"What's wrong, Miss Nashville? You hoping this is a dream or something?"

I open my eyes then and glare at him with absolute disgust. "If you leave now, I won't call the police."

He laughs. Only then do I realize that he's drunk.

"What makes you think I'm going to leave you in any shape to call the police?"

I feel a stab of fear then. "Rowdy, this isn't worth it. Leave now, and I won't tell anyone you were here."

"Ah, no, you see there are some things in this life," he says, each word bitten out, "that a man just can't sit back and take. One of those things is somebody robbing him of his own personal property."

"If you're talking about Brownie—"

"Killer," he interjects.

I refuse to acknowledge the name, but go on. "You're the one who shot him."

"And if you hadn't come out there, sticking your nose in my business, that would never have happened."

"Why do you even care, Rowdy? All you did was keep him tied up on a chain his whole life. It's not like you loved him."

"You don't love a dog. A man takes *pride* in his possessions."

"A dog can't be your possession," I say.

"The law of the state of Virginia says he can. I guess when you own something, it's your possession."

"Well, that's where the law's just wrong," I say. "One living being shouldn't own another."

"Maybe you're living a little out of your time, Miss High and Mighty. Maybe you should have been born a couple hundred years down the road. Because right now, in this country, I was the owner of my dog. And because of you, he's dead."

He's still holding me by my hair, his hand wound through it so that his fist is up tight against the back of my neck.

"One thing you can know for sure," he says, "is I ain't leaving until I get what I came for."

I know there's no way he could know about Brownie. But my heart is knocking hard against my chest anyway. He walks me over to one of the kitchen chairs, pushing me roughly onto the seat.

With one hand, he reaches in his pocket and pulls out a spool of plastic rope. He grabs my arm and then letting go of my hair, slams my wrists together and binds them behind the chair back with a rope.

My shoulders strain at the pressure, and I cry out, "Rowdy, you're hurting me!"

"Oh, I'm not done yet," he says. He reels off more rope and ties each of my legs to the chair, then wrapping more of the rope around my waist and the seat back.

"What are you doing?" I scream at him. "Rowdy, go! Please! Just leave. Now, while you still—"

"Shut up!" he yells at me. "I don't take orders from you or anybody for that matter."

He walks over to the refrigerator, opens the door and sticks his head inside, pulling out a beer and popping the top. He takes a long swig, holds the bottle out and looks at the label. "Fancy," he says.

The lights on the child monitor we keep on the kitchen counter blink. Lexie starts to cry through the intercom. It's soft at first, and I hear the fear in her crying.

"We must have woken her up," Rowdy says, sarcasm coating the words. "So sorry about that."

"Let me go to her," I plead. "She's scared. I'll just tell her everything is okay."

"But it's not," he says. "Okay, I mean."

"Rowdy, please stop this before you do something—"

"I'm gonna regret? Oh, I've got plenty of regrets. But here's the thing about regrets. A person can't go around dwelling on them all the time. You mess up, you take your licks, and you get back up and keep on going."

Lexie's crying is more persistent now. I hear her making the sound she uses for Mama. My heart feels as if it is being physically torn in half.

And then I hear the whine, followed by a distressed bark.

When the barking gets louder, I know Brownie has heard Lexie crying. I close my eyes against what's coming.

"Oh, you got yourself a dog, huh?" Rowdy says, walking to the door at the back of the kitchen and looking through the glass. I feel utterly sick as he steps back and yanks the door open, for once speechless.

At the sight of Rowdy, Brownie cowers, drops onto his belly, his head ducked as if he knows what's coming. Rowdy reaches out for his collar and yanks Brownie onto his hind legs.

"Are you shitting me?" he yells out. "You didn't kill my dog! You stole my dog!"

"He almost died! We just—"

He walks across the room, dragging Brownie by the collar, and backhands me across the face. I feel the pain explode inside my head. I cry out even as I try to fight it back.

Rowdy's face is so red, I think his head might blow right off his shoulders. He raises a boot and aims it at the center of my chest, shoving me backward so that the chair falls flat onto the hard kitchen floor.

I feel it knock the air from my chest, and for several seconds, I cannot breathe. Brownie yelps, and Rowdy roars at him to shut up. He reaches for the front of my pajamas, grabbing hard and yanking me straight up on the chair so that I am facing him again.

"You clearly need a little lesson here, so that you never again forget this dog is *my property*."

He pulls a pack of cigarettes from his shirt pocket. Knocking Brownie to the floor, he pins him there with his knee against his neck. As if he's lighting up for a casual smoke, he strikes the match, puts it to the tip of the cigarette, draws in a deep pull of smoke, and then blows it back out again.

The cigarette glows red hot. He holds it up to me as if to make sure I know exactly how hot it is and then leans over and starts to brand Brownie's side with burn marks, one by one by one, while tears roll down my face. I start to sob uncontrollably.

"Don't! Please, stop, Rowdy! Please, stop!"

But he doesn't.

He keeps going until the K is formed, the I, the L, L, E, R. And the name is there on his side.

Brownie never makes a sound. He just lies there still, as if he knows there's no escaping. And that this life he had here with us was always too good to be true.

♪

Thomas

Noise

NEW YORK CITY is just way too loud for me.

I went to bed around eleven-thirty, using much needed sleep as an excuse not to go to the party after tonight's show. But it was pretty much a wasted effort because I lie here on this plush five-star hotel bed, wide awake. And my thoughts are not here in this city with its constant traffic sounds and high-rise buildings.

My thoughts are at home. With Lila and Lexie and Brownie. I miss them. I'm homesick for them in a way I cannot deny. The roots of it are deep within me, and I want to go home, right now, on the very next flight.

I feel this pull I can't explain, but recognize all the same. I don't want to be away from them. All I've done since I got here, aside from when we're playing, is worry about whether they're all right. Whether Lila is managing everything on her own.

We're scheduled to leave in the morning, and I doubt that I could get a flight out before then anyway. But I need to hear her voice. I pick up my phone and dial her number, wondering what I'm going to say to her, whether I'll have the guts to just say the truth. *I miss you. I miss you so much.*

But the phone rings and rings. And there's no answer.

♪

Lila

Revenge

I AM CRYING so hard that I can barely see through my tears when Rowdy drags Brownie out of the kitchen and down the hallway to the front door. I hear it open and close and feel no relief for the fact that he's gone.

I jerk and tear at the ropes binding my arms and legs, screaming for help as loudly as I can, praying that someone will hear, that someone will come and help me get Brownie back before it's too late.

But then I hear the front door open again.

"Macy!" I scream out, willing it to be her.

There's no answer. I just hear Rowdy's heavy steps in the foyer. My heart stops as I scream at him. "What are you doing?!?"

I hear him walking again. Not this way toward me. But down the hall that leads to the bedrooms. From the monitor in Lexie's room, I hear the door click open, then the rustle of sheets. I start to cry again as I hear her fearful whimpers, the sound of Rowdy walking back across the floor.

"Come on, sugar," he says. "You and me are gonna take a little ride."

And then I'm screaming again, screaming, screaming until the sounds are being torn from me. I writhe and shake and jerk to no avail to get free, while he walks back down the hallway and out the front door, taking my daughter with him.

♪

Thomas

Fear

I HEAR THE PHONE ringing. It seems as if I just closed my eyes and fell asleep. I grapple for it on the nightstand next to the bed. I answer with a groggy, "Hello."

"Thomas?"

It's Macy, which I realize instantly, along with the fact that she is crying. I sit up in bed, running a hand across my eyes. "What is it, Macy? What's wrong?"

"Oh, Thomas." She's crying so hard that I can barely understand the words. "It's Lexie, and Brownie and Lila—"

"What's happened?" I sit there on the bed, completely still while she tells me. I hear what she's saying, but somehow the words won't process. It's as if my brain has gone numb and lost its ability to filter the words.

"Rowdy took them, Thomas. He just broke into the house and took them!"

"Are you saying that he kidnapped them?"

"Lexie and Brownie," she says, sobbing harder. "I'm at the hospital now with Lila."

"Let me speak to her, Macy! Please, now!"

"I can't. She's not really talking."

Fear crashes over me in a wave, slamming me so hard and with such force that I cannot find air to pull into my lungs. I don't even know what to ask first.

"You just need to get back here," Macy says. "As fast as you can."

"Are the police—"

"They're looking for him."

"Did he hurt them?"

"I don't really know, Thomas. Lila is . . . I guess she's in shock."

"Did he hurt her?"

"She has some cuts and bruises and a fairly bad knot on her head, but other than that, the doctors think physically she's fine. But she needs you here."

"I'll be there as soon as I can. My flight is at seven."

When we end the call, I sit, staring at the phone, unable to make myself move. I'm completely frozen with fear. My throat is swelling tight with it, as if I am having an anaphylactic reaction to some toxin I cannot physically deal with.

I'm scared to move, scared to look past this very moment into a future that might not turn out to be what I've been longing for it to be. I cannot even begin to imagine Rowdy hurting Lexie in any way.

But then I know what kind of man he is. What he did to Brownie. And that only a heartless person could do something like that. The thought of our child being at his mercy is beyond any definition of unbearable.

And suddenly, I'm bolting off the bed, running to the bathroom where I drop on my knees in front of the toilet and throw up. I have no food in my stomach, so there's nothing to come up. I gag hard.

Once the spasms stop, I drop back against the wall behind me. I have to get to Lila. I need to stand beside her, pull her into my arms and seal her to me. I think that is the only thing I can imagine giving me the strength to believe that we will find Lexie. That she'll be brought back to us, safe and unharmed.

I force myself to stand then. Start throwing my things into my bag. I'm out of the room in less than five minutes, making calls to get a private flight back to Nashville instead of waiting for my scheduled one.

I get a cab in front of the hotel, and since it's New York City, it's easy enough to do at this hour. It's still dark, and I stare out the window at the night sky. I find a single star to focus on. I don't take my eyes from it.

All the way to the airport, I pray. For Lila. For Lexie. For Brownie. I pray.

♪

Lila

Mortal Wound

I HAVE TO GET UP.

I hear Macy's question. Am I all right? I want to answer her. But I know as soon as I do, as soon as I speak, as soon as I move, I have to face what has happened.

I don't think I can. Not without breaking, cracking from the very center of my soul, the wound a mortal one. Because, truly, how can anyone survive this?

I know Macy is sitting next to me. I feel her fingers lace with mine. I feel too her grief and fear and let it meld with my own.

♪

I HEAR HIS footsteps in the hall outside the room before I ever see his face.

I know it's him by the sound of his boots on the hospital's hard floor. And then he's there, in the room, filling the doorway with his wide shoulders.

I look at his face, see reflected there what I feel inside. And it's only then that I start to cry.

Macy gets up, walks across the floor and puts a hand on Thomas's shoulder, tears running down her face. Without saying anything, she walks out of the room.

♪

Thomas

Brownie

I SIT ON THE chair next to Lila's bed, her hand locked between the two of mine. We're both crying with fully broken hearts. I know there's no one else in the world who can understand what Lila is feeling the way I do. Or how she understands that I'm feeling the very same thing.

"Please tell me they'll find her, Thomas. That they'll find both of them. That they'll be okay. Please tell me that."

"They'll find them, baby," I say.

"How do you know?" she asks, the words breaking at the end.

"I just know they will. I spoke with a detective right before I got to the hospital. They're doing everything possible to find them."

"What if they don't? What if she's hurt—"

"Baby, don't. Please don't. We just have to believe everything will be okay. That's our life raft. Just hold on to that. And I'll hold on to you."

She reaches for me then, opening her arms. I lift her up off the bed and onto my lap, wrapping her tight against me.

♪

A LITTLE OVER an hour later, a doctor comes in and okays Lila's release as long as I will be watching after her.

Macy is back in the room, and she helps Lila get dressed while I step out in the hallway.

My phone rings. I glance at the screen and recognize the number as the one belonging to the detective who had called me a little while ago. I answer quickly, my heart suddenly pounding so hard I can feel the pulse beat in my neck.

"Yes, detective, have you heard anything?"

I listen for several seconds. "Where?" I ask when she's done. "Where are they?"

"Mr. Franklin, I think it would be best if you—"

"Tell me where they are."

And I guess something in my voice convinces her to answer. Because she does.

"Thank you," I say, and then I'm running back in the room.

"Lila," I say. "They've found them. Come on, we have to go."

All the color drains from her face, and I can see her whole body go limp, as if she is about to fall. Macy grabs her just before I reach her side and sweep her into my arms.

I carry her like that, running through the hospital, into the parking garage where I put her in the truck. Macy is behind me, completely out of breath, but she's right there, jumping in the truck as I start it.

I hand Macy my phone and gun out of the garage, giving her the address. It's only a few miles from the hospital according to the GPS, but it still seems like it takes forever to get there.

I see the swarm of blue lights a quarter of a mile before we reach them. Traffic is stopped, cars lining up in front of us. There must be ten police units up ahead, all sitting at odd angles. Then I see the policemen with their guns pointed at the truck on the side of the road. Rowdy's truck.

When I realize I can drive no farther, I open the door and say to Lila and Macy, "Wait here, okay."

But neither one of them is having it. They're sliding out of the truck and running as hard as I am to get to the scene up ahead. As soon as we reach the patrol car, two policemen step up to stop us.

"I'm afraid you can't go past here," the taller one says, holding up a hand.

"I'm her father. And this is her mother," I say, putting a hand on Lila's arm. "Please. You have to let us go to her."

He looks at me for a moment, then says, "You're Thomas Franklin."

"Yes. And that's my daughter, Lexie, in the truck with that man."

"Hold on just a moment." He turns and says something into the phone on his shoulder. And then he looks at me and waves the three of us through.

He leads us to the center of the police barricade, introducing us to the head of the group.

The man looks at us with sympathetic eyes and says, "I'm Captain Jordan. A passerby saw the truck on the side of the road and called it in. He had heard about the search on the radio."

"Are they in there?" I ask.

"Yes. The suspect, a child and a dog."

"Lexie and Brownie are their names."

The captain nods once. "So far the suspect hasn't shown any willingness to come out."

"Please," Lila says, "promise me you won't do anything to get either of them hurt."

"Your daughter is our first priority," he says. He raises the megaphone in his left hand, directing it at the truck. "Mr. Maxwell," he calls out, using Rowdy's last name. "Considering where things are, the best choice you can make for yourself is to get out of that truck and turn yourself in. There's no way you're going to get out of this."

The truck window lowers a couple of inches. Rowdy yells, "Don't it look like I'm the one holding all the cards right here?"

"You do still have two innocent victims at your mercy, if that's what you mean," the captain says.

"Damn right," he throws back.

"Come out of that truck now, and prove to me that they're both okay, and we'll see what we can do about getting you a little leniency."

"Leniency, my ass! You think I don't know that's a crock of crap? I'm the one with all the power here."

Through the truck's back window, I see Rowdy's arm reach across and smack the back of Lexie's blonde head. I hear the growl, and then everything happens in an instant.

Brownie leaps onto Rowdy. The truck door opens, and Rowdy tumbles out on the pavement with Brownie on top of him. I see the awful word branded on his side. Killer.

The dog rolls Rowdy across the asphalt. He has him by the throat. Rowdy is squealing.

The police officers standing on either side of the captain raise their weapons, aiming at Brownie.

"No!" Lila screams. "Stop! Don't shoot him!"

And then she's running across the pavement, throwing herself between the officer's raised guns and Brownie where he had taken Rowdy down.

"Brownie!" Lila screams. "Stop! It's me! Brownie, stop! It's okay!"

When her voice finally penetrates, the dog goes still, as if he's been snapped from a trance. He shakes himself free of Rowdy's flailing arms and jumps back inside the truck.

Lila climbs in behind him, sobbing. I run to them, and as soon as I reach the truck door, I see her shielding both Lexie and Brownie inside the circle of her arms.

I open the passenger side door and pull all three of them to me. And if I could stand here, just holding them for the rest of my life, knowing they're okay, that they're still here with me, forever wouldn't be long enough.

♪

Lila

The Beginning

GRATEFUL IS A feeling.

But I have to wonder if it's a place as well. If so, I am firmly planted in the middle of it, and it's somewhere I never want to leave.

Thomas and I are in the living room, sitting side by side on the couch with Brownie. He's asleep next to me, his head on my lap.

CeCe and Holden left a few minutes ago, both of them visibly thankful that we are all okay. Macy went for coffee with Taylor after he called to find out what had happened. I suspect she wanted to give us some time alone. To be honest, I'm glad because I think Thomas and I are the only ones who can truly understand the relief we each feel.

"Should we go look at her again?" he asks now.

"She's all right," I say, even though I have his same desire to never take my eyes off her again.

I rub Brownie's ear. He sighs and stretches out longer on the sofa. "How do you think we'll ever thank him?" I ask.

"By making sure no one hurts him again and that he has the best life we can give him."

I see his gaze settle on the burn marks on Brownie's side. Just the memory of Rowdy's cruelty makes my stomach knot up.

"I can't even imagine what might have happened if he hadn't—"

"Don't," Thomas says, running the back of his hand across my hair. "Let's not do that. Lexie is okay. You and Brownie are okay. That's all that matters."

He's quiet for a moment before adding, "When I was waiting to fly home, I never imagined I could feel the way I felt, knowing I might lose everything that matters to me." He reaches over and takes my hand. "That's when I realized I can't picture my life without the two of you anymore. This thing we've been doing, acting like we don't care what the other one does, who the other one sees. It's not true for me, Lila. None of it. I do care. There's no one I want to be with other than you."

I hear the pure emotion in his voice, and tears well up in my eyes. My first response as always is to protect myself, keep the walls in place. Because if the wall is there and I don't let anyone over it, I can't be hurt.

But I know now that all of life is risk, and without risk, we can gain nothing. "I don't want to lose you," I say, looking down at our joined hands. "I don't want to lose us, this family we've been making when I didn't even realize it was that."

"But that is what we are, isn't it?" he says. "Today, facing the possibility of losing our daughter—"

"I know," I say. "It's unthinkable."

Thomas stands and then lowers himself onto one knee in front of me. He takes my other hand and locks his eyes with mine.

"Lila Bellamy, I love you. And I'm pretty sure I fell in love with you the first night we met. I know I love the child we made together. I don't want to live another day of my life without the two of you as my family. Will you be my wife? Will you marry me?"

I don't bother to try and stop the tears streaming down my face. They're tears of happiness, and I can only look at him and nod, my soft yes becoming a stronger, "Yes, yes, I will marry you. And yes, I love you. So very much."

I slide my arms around his neck and settle myself against him, closing my eyes and wondering just briefly if I deserve this happy ending.

But even as the thought passes through my mind, I realize it's not an ending at all.

It's just the beginning.

♪

Next: Nashville – Part Seven

Next: Nashville – Book Seven – Commit

THE NASHVILLE SERIES
BOOK SEVEN

commit

RITA® AWARD WINNING AUTHOR

INGLATH COOPER

Get in Touch With Inglath Cooper

Email: inglathcooper@gmail.com
   Facebook – Inglath Cooper Books
   Instagram – inglath.cooper.books
   Pinterest – Inglath Cooper Books
   Twitter – InglathCooper
   Join Inglath Cooper's Mailing List and get a FREE ebook! Good
Guys Love Dogs!

Made in the USA
Coppell, TX
07 May 2020